THE PICCADILLY

TWO THOUSAND GRUELING MILES
BOOK FOUR

L.J. MARTIN

WISE WOLF
BOOKS

WISE WOLF BOOKS
An Imprint of Wolfpack Publishing
wisewolfbooks.com

Cover design by Wise Wolf Books

ISBN 978-1-957548-93-7 (paperback) 978-1-957548-94-4 (hardcover)
978-1-957548-92-0 (ebook)

LCCN 2023942239

THE PICCADILLY

"You've aged well, Jake. What...now eighteen?" Lord Stanley-Smyth eyes me up and down like he's buying a fat steer to butcher.

"Yes, sir. Nineteen in two weeks."

"Over six feet and fifteen stone I'd guess."

"Fifteen stone, sir?"

"Sorry, well over two hundred pounds and not an ounce of fat."

I must smile. I've been at sea working for Stanley-Smyth for over two years, and climbing the ratlines of an oceangoing full-rigged ship is not a job encouraging a generous girth. I've gained weight, but it's muscle, gristle, and bone—not fat. And I've gained even more confidence than weight. I'd come to San Francisco, as they say, wet behind the ears. Facing hard men on the streets of the wild and woolly gold rush town and working with them in the sheets and shrouds of three different ships will do that for a fella. If I didn't have confidence sixty feet high over a pitching wave-washed deck, standing on a half-inch line in force five gales, gathering sail, I'd soon be ten times that deep in the briny, polishing the silver in Davy Jones's locker.

"Please have a seat. Have you developed a taste for liquor?"

"Grog, of course, or my mates onboard would have doubted my manhood. A touch of whiskey in port but I've always tried to keep my wits about me."

"I'll pour us a dram of the Highland's best. I have a proposal for you."

"Highlands?"

"Scotland, the tears of the peat bogs. Scotch, young man. A gentleman's drink."

"Thank you."

"Take a seat."

I do, and immediately a yellow, long-haired cat jumps into my lap.

The Lord laughs. "That's the missus's cat, Mugsy. She seems to miss the missus as much as I do." He places my three fingers of Scotch in front of me, then adds, "She doesn't take to most men. Seems she's a fine judge of character."

I give her a scratch behind the ears and she purrs.

We're in the finest hotel in San Francisco, the Niantic. She started out as one of the many abandoned ships winched up onshore and added to as demand grew, then burned, and since rebuilt as most of San Francisco has done more than once. From 1849 to 1851 over eight hundred vessels were abandoned by crews clamoring to reap the riches of the goldfields. Now only a few dozen remain. Most of the former had not sailed away but rather were stripped of all useful for constructing the city.

I take a seat in a red velvet armchair across a highly polished walnut desk in the Lord's hotel suite. Behind his facing chair, high on the wall, is the portrait of his wife. I know he lost his wife while I was somewhere on the China coast aboard the *Orient Flyer*, one of the Lord's growing fleet.

He hands me a crystal goblet with three fingers of whisky, and I toast him, or more correctly his late wife. "I was so very sorry to hear of Lady Stanley-Smyth's passing, so if I may, to her memory, sir."

He clinks glasses with me, saying nothing, and I believe he chokes up a little, then clears his throat. "She thought very highly of you, Jake."

"Sir, she was like a second mother to me, if in a distant sort of way. I wouldn't admit this to any other man, but I wept when I heard of her passing."

I get a sincere smile from him, and another toast. His voice almost cracks again as he speaks. "When you went back into the desert and fetched our son's body home, you found a place in her...in both our hearts." Then he laughs, and adds, "When she was alive, I would have never undertaken my current purchase."

"Sir?"

"I've bought the Bucket of Blood Saloon and Bawdy House down on the Barbary Coast, and I want you to jump ship from the *Orient* and take on the job of looking over my interest there."

I'm taken aback and silenced for a moment as he studies my reaction.

I clear my throat before responding. "I admit I have been in a sporting house, sir, but never had an inkling I might be employed in one."

He laughs. "It's often part of a young man's education, although not one likely to be reported to one's sainted mother."

I smile tightly. "And I have not and will not do so."

The smile is returned before he continues. "I intend to change the name to The Piccadilly so as not to appeal to quite so rough a clientele. And the so-called bawdy house will become the West's finest bordello. But the business will still be based on the same sound money-making propositions. Gambling, liquor, and the more sublime pleasures of the flesh."

Again, I'm silent a moment, then must speak my mind. "Sir, I could be a part of the former, gambling and liquor, but taking advantage of the weaker sex...I'd not be welcome in my mother's house should she even suspect me..."

"Of running a brothel," he says, with a chuckle, then adds, "You won't be running either the saloon or the brothel. I've hired a competent manager as well as a man handy with a six-gun for the saloon and gambling, and a renowned madam, who I met long before my wife. She's on her way from Mexico City, possibly bringing some Latin beauties to join our Celestials. Your job will be to set shotgun in the saloon on the nights needed, possibly to protect some of the weaker sex, and to see that the income is actually truthfully reported. Otherwise, you'll be sort of my eyes, roving about, overlooking all, seeing the money goes in the till, not a pocket."

I smile and shake my head. "Sir, I know nothing of running a saloon and very little about gambling. I'm a fair hand at cribbage and have played a little poker..."

"And you'll soon learn the intricacies of faro, the most popular and prolific game played in city saloons, and brag, three-card monte, and dice games such as high-low, chuck-a-luck, and grand hazard."

"Sitting shotgun sounds like little more than guard and gunman?"

"In this case it's much more, Jake. You'll learn business as you'd never do, even trading as you have done on the *Orient*. There will be a hundred transactions of a dozen types going on all around you every hour of every night. And you'll have two dozen or more employees… and yes, the two managers, to watch carefully. At closing you'll count the take alongside the two managers and note the totals and see the take is deposited in our new Victor safe. The business is famous for cheats, and I don't condone cheating but handsomely reward those who protect my interests…and that'll be you if you choose to accept? You'll be my eyes and ears."

"You've always been more than fair, sir. I hope I can be of service to you, but I swear, this seems a real stretch from seaman to sittin' shotgun, to watching for cheats when I don't know fair play—"

"Let's go see if the chef has a couple of beef steaks and talk some more. You've always been a fast student, Jake, and you will be here as well. And it's five dollars a day and found, with the possibility of a bonus. You'll have a garret room with maid service…a far cry from folding into a five-foot bunk below decks."

I have to laugh at that, then agree, "Getting to sleep stretched out might be worth the change." It's what I say, but what I think is that I can send at least fifty dollars a month home to my ma in Oregon.

When the ship docked from China, I had a half-dozen letters awaiting me, the last of which informed me of the death of my stepfather, Captain Quinton Haroldson, which leaves the farm to be tended by my brother-in-law and my good friend Sampson. And they both have their own to care for. Fifty dollars a month will hire a man to do Ma's hard work. So, it's either return to the farm or do what's likely better for all of us, and that's see where this new opportunity takes me.

My mother taught us many things, making my sisters and I learn a new word each day from a dictionary she carried the near two thousand miles along the Oregon Trail, and that understanding of language has served me well. She also taught us the lessons of the Bible, which she studied with an open mind and understanding it was written centuries ago. She knew its contradictions and instructed us to take the best from it. And with this opportunity presented me by Lord Stanley-Smyth, I can't help but remember a couple of passages. One, as I recall from Matthew, "Jesus said to them, 'The tax collectors and the prostitutes are going into the Kingdom of God ahead of you. For John the Baptist came to you showing you the right path to take, and you would not believe him; but the tax collectors and the prostitutes believed him.'"

I'm not sure about the tax collectors, but I imagine most ladies of the night are in that profession, if it can be called a profession, due to the unfortunate circumstances of their lives. Maybe working near I can in some way better their circumstance. If not that, then they do the work for pure greed for gold. I hope I can resist the temptation of working daily with women who'll share their favors. I can see where one might be tempted to not only take advantage but be taken in by charms shared out of hope for advantage, not true caring. The Bible also says, Proverbs if memory serves, "...for the lips of a prostitute are as sweet as honey, and smooth flattery is her stock in trade. But afterwards only a bitter conscience is left to you, sharp as a double-edged sword."

Setting shotgun and being the conscience of a saloon and to some extent, I imagine, a bawdy house, will, sure as hell's hot, be an education. And one I'll be paid to receive rather than pay to obtain. That said, it also seems like a grand place to get a belly full of lead, or, if tempted beyond restraint, the pox.

I will, if you'll pardon the pun, gird my loins, and look with interest and an open mind upon my scheduled morning visit to the currently being remodeled Bucket of Blood. I don't think I can afford to turn down the financial opportunity. I hope it's not blood money.

2

I SLEEP LATE AND WELL IN A NIANTIC HOTEL BED—
probably my last here as I'm told I'm moving to quarters
in The Piccadilly—and courtesy of Lord Stanley-Smyth,
have my breakfast in the hotel dining room, just
finishing as his lordship enters. He joins me and I
quickly beg to be excused. "Sir, I'd like to wander the
waterfront a bit then meet you at the Bucket of—"

"The Piccadilly, if you don't mind."

"Yes, sir. The Piccadilly, in say an hour. Eight o'clock
sharp?"

"My coach and driver are outside. Take it and pick
me up here at eight."

"I'd as soon wear some leather off'n these new
brogans you brought me, if you don't mind. I'm enjoying
having my land legs under me."

"Eight o'clock, sharp."

"Yes, sir."

Only a few blocks to the ever-expanding waterfront,
and downhill all the way. Shops, cafés, and saloons that
were waterfront when I'd left the city a year ago are now

facing new shops, cafés, and saloons on fill that continues to extend the city where the bay had been. The streets seem as full as when I departed—drays, buggies, coaches, freight wagons, and a few horsebackers crowd the road planks and most of the ships; barks and brigs that had been winched ashore to serve as buildings are gone or remodeled so much it is hard to tell what the origin had been.

The streets are also filled with the same eclectic bunch of folks as when I left aboard the *Orient*. Chinese, Mexicans, Peruvians, Englishmen, Germans, Italians, and the ever-present Australians in the form of gangs of Sydney Ducks lurk about or go about their sordid business...although I see none of the Wallaby gang I'd tangled with before sailing off. Hopefully they've made their ill-gotten fortune and departed for the barrier reef and the outback. I'd blown the left leg off their leader and he'd put a five-hundred-dollar bounty on my head, luckily no one collected before I sailed away.

Hopefully no one will collect now that I'm back, presuming the bounty still stands.

The city has grown, and folks come and go and I hope all those former folks are long gone. It's said well over a hundred thousand Argonauts have passed through San Francisco on their way to the diggings in the many months I've been gone, and some have stayed to work the miners rather than work the mines and nooks and crannies of the rivers and streams.

So, I am not surprised when I see no one I know. The *Orient Flyer* has sailed to trade up and down the coast and the *Windsong*, the lumber ship I'd served aboard prior to being moved to the trans-Pacific full-rigged ship, is off up the coast to procure another profitable load of building materials.

I end my inspection of the new waterfront and find my way to the Bucket of Blood, not surprised to see a gold leaf lettered sign over a dozen feet wide, *The Piccadilly*, with a Union Jack painted on each end, flanking the name. Three stories of sturdy brick painted white, a red door and window trim. It appears she's about ready to open. I wait by the batwing doors in front of ten-foot-high, heavy double doors, one of which sports a smaller gold leaf sign, *The Piccadilly*, the other one of equal size, informs *Alice's Pleasure Parlor* with smaller letters below, *Exotic Company for Every Gentleman's Taste*. I am just about to decide this job is not for me, when the Lord's coach arrives and he steps down as I step forward, to tell him I want my job back aboard the *Orient Flyer*, when he turns and offers a helping hand to the most beautiful woman I've ever seen.

Sweeping long blond hair back over a shoulder with one hand, she offers the Lord the other. She gracefully steps out of the buggy. He turns and as I am tongue-tied, introduces us. "Jake Zane, please greet Miss Alice Deschamps, formerly of New Orleans, the last few years of Mexico City."

She eyes me with emerald eyes, extends a hand to shake like a man, and I am taken aback and look like the dunce I feel myself to be. I finally collect myself as her hand stays extended, and shake, as gently as I can muster. I don't believe a woman has ever extended a hand to shake upon being introduced or any other time.

"Ma'am, my pleasure," I manage.

"You come highly recommended, Mr. Zane. Lord Stanley-Smyth says I'm to ignore your youth as you've experienced more than many three times your age. I'm to rely upon you." She gives me a devastating smile, then asks, "So, Mr. Jake Zane, can I rely on you?"

"Of course, ma'am. I was taught to respect and protect women."

"Even women in my trade?" Her look hardens.

"Ma'am, a woman in a hardscrabble dugout on the prairie or a woman in a French palace. I was taught to respect women, no matter their station in life."

She laughs a little twitter that is as ladylike a laugh as I've ever heard, then manages, "What a sweet boy you are. It's hard to imagine you've faced savages and Sydney Ducks and half the riffraff of the world and still seem as gentle as a lamb."

Lord Stanley-Smyth has enjoyed this exchange, if his smile is an indicator and offers, "He's had enough blood on his hands to assure both of us he'll have no trouble looking out for our interests, no matter what it requires. Now, let's take a look at the facilities."

The Lord holds the door for us and holds up just inside. He points upstairs at a balcony. "Alice, your facilities are off the landing above. No one enters your bordello from the street. All must pass through the saloon under the scrutiny of our bouncers and also young Jake here."

She looks puzzled. "I was told there is a special entrance for those who don't want to be seen?"

"There is, but only for select well-vetted customers. Townsmen, politicians, bankers, professional men who are well checked out and have impeccable manners, and of course don't want their proclivities known, particularly to their customers and wives." Then he guffaws, and adds, "We'll exit that way after our tour."

The main room of the saloon is the same size as when it was the Bucket of Blood, thirty feet or so wide and maybe twice that deep. What surprises me is the ceiling height. Nearly every customer in a saloon is smoking a cigar or pipe, so normally you can't see ten feet for the smoke. This room is at least eighteen feet high with a balcony covering the last third of the floor space, it's twenty feet or so deep. On the west side of the balcony is a pair of double doors which we soon learn leads to the building on that side, all of which is the bordello. The balcony has a six-foot radius quarter round extending over the bar below, which is at least forty feet long with a backbar lined with mirrors and bottle shelves, except for a ten-foot square that sports a massive eight-foot-square painting of a lady nearly as beautiful as Miss Alice…only not nearly so clothed. She reclines on a red sofa wearing as few garments as when she was delivered into the world. As I stare at the painting then turn to see the sly smile on Miss Alice's face, I feel my cheeks go warm and color.

"You are a charming lad," she says, with a laugh, and heads for the stairway opposite the bar leading up to the balcony. She threads through gambling tables as if right at home, and I guess she is if she's worked New Orleans and Mexico City. We follow as she glides up the stairway, not bothering to grasp the carved and polished handrail.

As I follow the Lord, I can't help but compliment him. "I was only here a couple of times with the crew, but I wouldn't recognize the place. I believe you've torn the first floor off thus doubling the ceiling height and replaced the plank bar and backbar with the finest I've ever seen. A brass rail and brass spittoons where crockery used to serve. Mirrors behind each shelf and glasses and pewter mugs rather than tin cups and clay mugs. New tables and upholstered chairs. Felt-covered gaming tables. Painted walls…"

"You're very observant, Jake. And we have the finest

wines and liquors from the world over. As you'll soon learn, our clientele is just that as well, the finest, and we'll tolerate no fisticuffs or gunplay. And the games are honest...the odds of each are with the house so there's no reason to push them our way. You're to see they stay honest."

"Can we see the pleasure side," Miss Alice asks, obviously eager to see if it is the finest as well.

"The bordello building was a mixed-use structure, chandlery below and boarding rooms on the two floors above, now we have a salon with a small bar, indoor privies that feed into tanks in the cellar below, and two baths tended by Celestial girls." He opens one of the double doors and stands aside so we can enter.

"We'll start below," he says, and descends a stairway. This time Miss Alice floats down between us.

Where the walls of the saloon are natural brick, these are papered in a patterned red seeming to have a felt-like surface, the same pattern as the pounded, silver-colored tin ceilings. "There's a stairway both up to the balcony and through a door, down to a cellar that has quarters for Abe, our swamper, storage for supplies, and tanks for the toilets above. Abe's most offensive job is shoveling and bucketing those tanks, which are delivered up a rear stairway to the alley, and tank wagons to be hauled off and dumped into the bay."

We gather at the foot of the stairs and he points to the rear. "Another stairway leads to the cellar with living quarters below and garrets in the attic for housing the girls. The rooms were very small but now two have become one, with a double bed and a settee with two chairs, a dozen rooms for business. Of course, there's a table with pitcher and bowl for cleanliness's sake. I've made arrangements with Dr. Phinias Southerby, only a half block away, who'll inspect the ladies weekly, or more if called upon. We'll have the cleanest and fanciest bordello this side of the Mississippi."

"Now," Miss Alice says with a coy smile, "I see why you say we'll charge two dollars a token, twice that of other houses."

"And possibly more. We'll have the finest ladies in the land. No man will be entertained if he smells of the gutter or the fishing boats. The baths are a requirement, not a luxury for such as them and the bath is another dollar.

"Are you pleased?" he asks Miss Alice.

"As punch," she replies.

"And you, Jake." He turns to me.

I clear my throat. "Not my duty station, sir. However, the saloon and gambling facilities are as fine as any I've seen here or over the Pacific."

"That little quarter round on the balcony over the bar…"

"I noticed it," I say.

"That's your duty station. When not cruising the rooms, you'll look over the bar and gambling and be the last line of defense guarding the doors into Miss Alice's domain. Of course, we'll have a man at the front doors, a man at the stairway, and a man in the parlor of the bordello. At least that's my recommendation. But you'll do as you think right. I let my managers make their own mistakes." He gives me what I think is a cunning smile.

I clear my throat again. "I don't know, sir, I—"

"Hold on, Jake, you haven't seen your quarters yet. Follow me."

We return to the balcony and he leads me across to a door I hadn't noticed, and opens it to a narrow hallway. Inside are two doors, one to the front side and one the back. He opens the one to the back and I follow him in, not a single room but a two-room apartment. The living room is five times the size of my tiny cabin aboard the *Orient*. It has a bedroom large enough for the bed that would sleep four men, a settee, and a piece of furniture serving as a closet. There's a door to a small deck outside with a tiny stall at one end, a privy with a chute dropping all the way to the cellar. Next to the seat is a bucket with scoop, full of lye to treat the chute and tank below. A more pleasant subject is kitchen area in the main room with a pie cabinet and small table seating two.

He laughs at my incredulous look. "Not big enough?"

"How many of us live here?" I ask.

"Just you, Mr. Zane, just you." I'm speechless, so he closes me. "When can you move in?"

I could sail the world over and never afford something like this, all this and five dollars a day and good food from the saloon kitchen.

I shrug. "I left a few things in my room at the Niantic. When do we open for business?"

He nods. "Within the next fortnight. We've an advertisement in both city newspapers and will begin hiring tomorrow. Tennessee Tom Throckmorton is due on this evening's ferry from Benicia. Let's meet him and all go to supper."

"And he is?" I ask.

"He's the manager of the saloon and gambling parlor. He'll have another man under him, Colt Barberosa, who's arriving tomorrow on the *Benicia Belle* side-wheeler. Colt's been running rooms on the Mississippi and Sacramento. It seems he came by his nickname, Colt, due to its application ofttimes. Said to be a man of few words." Lord Stanley-Smyth guffawed, enough so the tips of his gray handlebar mustache bounced, as if he found that more than a little amusing. "Then I'm off to Washington D.C., New York, and possibly London, and will leave it to you four. We'll talk bonuses when I return, if you've kept the Piccadilly alive...by the way, I'm not fond of the ownership of The Piccadilly being known, so keep it under your hat." Then he turns to Miss Alice, "And I guess more pointedly, under your bonnet." Again, he laughs.

I can't help but ask. "And this Tennessee Tom...he's my boss?"

"I'm the only boss you have, Jake. You're your own man here at The Piccadilly...you can make suggestions, but not demands, and they can't demand anything of you."

"So, I'm to report to you. Looks to me like I'll be suspect at all times. Not the best way to make friends with the help."

He smiles. "You're tough enough to be disliked. I want them to respect you, not merely win your favor."

3

THE SIDE-WHEELER *BENICIA BELLE* TIED UP AND DROPPED her gangplanks right on time. Forward, nearest the mainland, is a three-foot-wide passenger gangway. Aft is one twice that wide for freight and stock. As we await Tennessee Tom Throckmorton, a six-up of fine-looking coal-black mules are being off-loaded, and for the first time since I landed in San Francisco, I see someone I recognize, easy to spot as he still wears a plainsman's buckskins and fur hat.

Some over a year ago Obadiah Barnabas—a stranger to me—had come along the boardwalk at exactly the right time. I was, foolishly, not heeled and found myself facing three Wallabys, from one of the worst Sydney Duck gangs. Three who had a major bone to pick with me as I'd put my Sharps to good use and sent five of their mates to meet their maker...or more likely Satan...as they were robbing the shipment of gold I'd ushered all the way from Oregon. Lord Stanley-Smyth's gold, the success of which was the first of my tasks that endeared me to him and his Lady. Barnabas had pushed his way between the three hooligans and passed me close enough I could relieve him of the Colt he carried and relieve the Colt of a chunk of lead into the knee of the worst of the Wallabys. That gang leader was later to have the leg sawed off from the knee down. A loss which resulted in his putting a bounty on my head.

I'd been helpful in getting Barnabas, Obey I soon labeled him, a job with Lord Stanley-Smyth, but that was over a year ago so I'm surprised to see him here.

I step away from the Lord and Miss Alice and harken Barnabas. "Obey, old friend, you're a sight for sore eyes." And I walk toward him. He stares a moment in the failing light, then brays like one of the mules he has gathered on the dock.

"By the saints, is that young Jake Zane I see?" He strides forward, then stops short. "And by all that's holy it's my employer." He turns his attention to the Lord. "Did you come to check on me, sir?"

The Lord shakes his head and steps forward and extends his hand. "I didn't expect you for a day or two, but glad you're here and see you've found some fine-looking stock."

"Yes, sir. This brace will pull your freight up the steepest grade and be ready for more."

"Lord Stanley-Smyth," a voice rings out from the passenger gangway and the Lord breaks away from us and extends a hand to the tall well-dressed man in frock coat, top hat, brocaded waistcoat, and four-in-hand tie. And Tom is not alone. On a leash is a hound that must weight near a hundred pounds, a long gray-haired critter, which, I'm happy to note, is wagging his tail.

"Throckmorton, I presume," the Lord says as they shake.

"At your service, sir," he says, but he's eyeing Miss Alice as he shakes.

The Lord quickly adds, "And this is Miss Alice Deschamps and Jake Zane, a protégé of mine."

He shakes my hand, but as before has eyes only for Miss Alice. He drops my hand and bows as he picks her gloved hand up and passes it near his lips and smacks a small kiss without actually touching the back of her hand.

She nods, "My pleasure."

And he speaks what I know to be French. *"Enchante,"* which I think means enchanted. The Lord doesn't bother to introduce Barnabas but turns to him. "You know where the Kingdom Stable is?"

"No, sir."

"Eight blocks up and two east back toward the bay. I own the place which is the new headquarters of Kingdom Freight and Mail. Max is the hostler and he'll find a dry stall where you can bed down. Don't waste time." His voice is officious and a little harsh and he gives his back to Obey. I haven't seen him with other employees and am thinking I'm fortunate we have a personal as well as employee-employer relationship. Then my opinion changes as he stops Barnabas with, "By the way, the manager's job at Kingdom is open if you want it. I'll be along tomorrow to talk it over with you."

Barnabas looks a little surprised, then replies, "I'll be there, sir."

The Lord eyes the big hound, then asks, "And this monster is?"

Tom gives him a bit of a doubting look, as if he thinks the Lord doesn't approve, but answers, "Irish wolfhound, name's Tor. He took to me a couple of years ago and when he takes to you, you'd better consider it a blessing.

I should have warned you, I guess. Where I go, Tor goes. We're a team."

The Lord gives him a nod and a slight shrug, so I guess Tor is accepted. He smiles and scratches the dog's ears before speaking, then looks up. "So long as he doesn't feed on our customers, or scare them off. Our coach awaits," he says, and leads off.

Before I follow, I catch Obey's eye. "I'm expected to join them or I'd buy your supper. I'll find this Kingdom Stable and buy breakfast. Sunup?"

"See you before the sun clears the East Bay mountains," he says with a laugh.

We're halfway down the dock to the coach when another voice rings out, and this one gruff and demanding.

"Gambler, you're not running like a by God skunk. You got my hard-earned and you're giving it back."

We all stop and turn to see a man only twenty feet behind. He's beer barrel big and standing with legs spread, one eye squinted half closed, his brow furrowed, the corn-cob-size index finger he's pointing at Tom is twitching nervously, and a six-gun hanging at one side in a ham-size paw bounces up and down like it's about to be raised to center on Tom's fancy waistcoat.

Tennessee Tom has spun around, frock coat open with a hand resting on a Sheriff's Colt at his side. His hound suddenly growls and lunges, but Tom has him on a tight leash.

I quickly place a hand on Miss Alice's back and guide her to the edge of the dock, waterside, away from the line of fire should worse come to worse. And call to the Lord. "Come this way, sir," and he promptly follows.

Tom is standing, one foot slightly in front of the other. I notice he's facing the man but offering a smaller target than if he was front on. He's not drawing, but hoisting the Sheriff's Model slightly, making sure it's riding free and easy in its polished black leather holster. His voice is calm and steady. "Sir, …Mr. Jenkins as I recall, when you lose at poker it is no longer your 'hard-earned.' It's now my property and I'd suggest you accept that as your misfortune and none of my own."

But the big interloper continues, "And I think you're a cheating som'bitch so take your hand off'n that little pissant firearm and reach slow-like and fetch me my money. And control that mutt or I'll put one twixt them yellow eyes."

To my surprise, Tom gives him both hands, palm out and lets his coat cover the Sheriff's Model. "It's your destiny, Mr. Jenkins." He reaches with his left hand up as if to retrieve a wallet from the inside, right side, pocket of the frock coat.

He comes out with a two-barrel pocket gun, looking to be a thirty-six caliber or larger, cocking it as it comes. He's caught Jenkins by surprise and the man hesitates a half second too long, only having his heavy revolver raised slightly when the pocket gun roars and spits flame. Even at twenty feet Tom's aim is accurate with the little weapon and he's hit Jenkins in the throat. Jenkins's revolver is slung aside as he drops to his knees and grasps his throat with both hands, blood pumping between his fingers. The way his legs folded I'd guess the shot severed his spine at the back of his neck as even his arms go limp as he pitches forward on his face.

Tom calmly repockets the derringer and walks the few paces over to where we stand, all seemingly speech-less. The big dog is emitting a low growl, but his atten-tion is at the big lout bleeding out on the wharf's rough timbers.

Tom faces Miss Alice, "I'm sorry you had to see that, Miss Deschamps. Had I not been forced…" Striding over he bends over the big man and shakes his head. "Mercy, I was aiming twixt his pig eyes. I'll have to work on my gunmanship."

She clears her throat, where she has one hand clasping her own as if to stop Jenkins's hurt. Then she nods, calm, but her voice an octave higher than normal. "Nothing I haven't seen before, Mr. Throckmorton." She turns to the Lord. "Do we have to await the authorities or can we proceed to supper. I'm famished."

The Lord lets out a long wheeze as if he's been holding his breath. He shakes his head and turns to me. "Damn if this is not a bloody land. Jake, I'll send the coach back for you to join us when you're through with the police. Have Barnabas wait to back up your testimony. Tell the coppers we're at Desmond's Delmonico if they need additional witnesses or want a statement from Tom, but not to bother us for a couple of hours to give us a chance to supper in peace. Watson P. Willowby is city marshal now and the federal admiralty judge is Ogden Hoffman…who you've met if you recall. Use their names if the coppers give you any trouble. We'll have a seat for you. Hope this doesn't take too much time."

"I'll take care of things, sir. I'll see you soon." And, as Tom lifts the hound up next to a doubting driver, I turn back to find Obey, who's on one knee next to the now dead man.

"He's goin' cold as a horseshoe," he says to me, shaking his head.

Behind him stand a half-dozen mules, snorting and shaking their heads. Obey sees me eying them and offers, "Mules is damn smart. They know the scent of blood is trouble. I'm surprised they ain't bolted with the noise and all and dragged me halfway to Monterey."

"Had you met this Jenkins?" I ask.

"I watched the game for a few hands. Even if the old boy who shot him could cheat, he didn't need to. This ol' boy was a rube. Even I could take his money. I'll bet the shooter—"

"Tennessee Tom," I offer.

"Even if this Tom fella wasn't so tricky with that hideout gun, I'd bet Jenkins couldn't have hit his own toe had he been aiming from two feet. He was drunk as a toad in a whiskey barrel. Had been drinking and bemoaning his losses for the last hour."

"Well," I say, with a shrug, "you can't blame Mr. Throckmorton. Even a drunk toad can get lucky." I eye the man, no longer blowing blood. "He ain't moaning no more. You gotta wait, the Lord's instructions, and back me up with the tales we'll be telling the coppers."

As other passengers filter by, each giving Jenkins a long look, a few removing their hats as they pass, I look up and see two coppers on the run coming our way.

Obey is calming his mules when they reach us and the taller of the two, a red-headed, rawboned, hard-eyed fella snaps at me, "What the hell happened here?"

Somehow, I'll bet I'm going to miss my fancy supper.

4

HE'S ADDRESSING OBEY BUT KNOWING HOW ROUGH-speaking the plainsman is, and that I want to finish this as quickly as possible as the promise of a meal at Desmond's Delmonico, the cities most renowned eatery, is a treat I'd hate to miss. So, I answer, "This fellow, Jenkins I heard him called, drew his weapon on the wrong opponent. It seems he'd lost his poke while aboard the side-wheeler there. Seems he met with a luckier, or more skilled, poker player."

"So, this poker player has fled? Does he have a name?"

"Yes, sir. Throckmorton, Tom Throckmorton."

"Tennessee Tom Throckmorton?"

"Yes, sir. I was just introduced to him but that seems his handle."

"He's a shootist of some repute. So, we'll have a company—"

"No, sir, he's gone to Desmond's Delmonico to partake of his evening meal. Seems Lord Stanley-Smyth, my employer and Throckmorton's employer, had a reservation and said they couldn't wait."

"Bullshit, kill a man and not wait on the authorities?" He turns to his mate, "Alexander, let's go jerk this poker player out of Delmonico's and take him in for a statement and possible booking."

"Sir," I say quickly, "I'm sure Mr. Throckmorton will be pleased to meet with your employer, Willowby, or Judge Hoffman at a decent hour tomorrow—"

"What the hell do you know of my boss or the federal judge?"

"No matter, sir. But I'd suggest you check with Marshal Willowby before you embarrass yourself and Lord Stanley-Smyth. You have my word Mr. Throckmorton will appear at your headquarters by ten a.m. tomorrow."

"And I should take your word?" He's sneering at me.

"I'm acting for Lord Stanley-Smyth, and, yes, you should take our word."

He's silent for a long moment, eying me as, since I'm off to supper with the Lord, I'm dressed in my only city suit of clothes which has this long year been stored at the Niantic. Then he finally speaks. "And where's your abode?"

"The Niantic, sir. I'm in residence at the Niantic."

"And your name?"

"Jake Zane. Please check with the desk."

"Then walk there with me," he commands, still wondering who the devil I am.

"I suggest we await Lord Stanley-Smyth's coach, which is due back shortly, and we can ride there before I go to join his party at Delmonico's."

He's now totally taken aback, and nods thoughtfully. Then relents, "No need. Make sure this Throckmorton is at Marshal Willowby's office ten a.m. sharp."

"Thank you. May I ask your name?"

"I'm police Sergeant Zeb O'Madden."

"And I'll be in some authority at the recently remodeled Bucket of Blood, and if you and your mates care to call on The Piccadilly—I'm sure you've seen the new sign —I'd be proud to stand you to a few rounds of good Irish and a beefsteak."

This brings a smile that nearly touches his ears, and his mate, Alex, a tall thin fella with a prominent Adam's apple, long limbs, and bony rough hands that testify he may have been a mason or lumberjack at some past time, crowds up as well and extends his still-calloused hand, "Officer Alex O'Toole, at your service."

"We should be open by the first of the week, gentlemen. Look forward to your calling on us."

O'Madden turns to O'Toole. Removing his billed officer's hat, he scratches his pate under a full head of Irish-red hair, then with great authority commands, "Get the digger and get this trash off the docks."

O'Toole hurries away just as Lord Stanley-Smyth's coach arrives.

"Can I give you a lift anywhere?" I ask.

"No, sir. I'm on duty here at the docks. But I'll be around to collect that Irish dew soon enough."

"And I'll look forward to seeing you. We'll run an honest place and the police are always welcome."

With that, I wave goodbye to Obey and am, finally, off to my fancy supper.

Dismounting the coach, I must stand motionless for a moment and admire the entrance to the city's most renowned eatery. I'm sure I'm in the right place as tied to a stanchion, a railing guarding a pit with windows on the floor or cellar below, is Tom's big hound. Double doors of polished walnut are framed by more than three dozen cut-glass panes in windows equally high as the doors.

The doors themselves each have an oval pane nearly three feet tall, and each with a *D* cut into the glass. As I'm dismounting from as fine a mode of transportation as is in all of San Francisco—maybe all of California—the doorman doesn't hesitate to hold the door for me. I give him a smile and nod as if this is a normal occurrence. Upon entering I find myself in a foyer, the second set of doors are open, I presume closed only during inclement weather. Just inside, flanking the entry, are two Chinese vases at least five feet tall, and palms rise from them another five feet. The room is not as large as I suspected, four round tables down the center, seating eight, and the walls lined with tables—five to a side—each inside its only little polished walnut cubicle, seating four each. The cubicles have dark curtains that can be closed for privacy…I presume for business meetings or more likely assignations.

I spot my party, in the last table closest to the double swinging doors which I presume lead to the kitchen, easily deduced as waiters dressed in starched white shirts with black four-in-hand ties, black coats and trousers, flow in and out with trays held shoulder high. Steaming trays exit, trays with bused tableware entering.

Lord Stanley-Smyth rises and waves me on. I stride their way, removing my hat as I come. A waiter slows me, "Hat, sir," and I hand it over.

"Hope you don't mind," the Lord says, having retaken his seat. "We started without you. So, how'd it go with San Francisco's finest?"

He motions me to a seat between himself and Tennessee Tom, across from Miss Alice, and I greet them with a nod before taking it.

"So?" the Lord presses.

"A bit hostile at first, but when mentioning their boss

and the judge, then seeing your coach arrive to fetch me away, their attitude changed. That said, I'm to appear at the marshal's office first thing in the morning with Mr. Throckmorton to give our statements."

"And Barnabas?"

"The copper didn't mention him, but I'll bring him along if you think it wise."

"I do. Advise them I'll come along later in the morning with Miss Deschamps, to verify all your testimony. That should settle the matter."

"Humph," was all the comment Tennessee Tom could muster. Then he added, "I don't need an escort. I'll show up on my own."

"As you wish," I say, with a nod.

I'm barely seated before a bowl containing a half-dozen raw, shucked oysters are placed in front of me, with a fork barely large enough to hold a pea residing among them, poked into a half lemon.

The Lord addresses the waiter. "Bring my young friend a flute," he instructs.

I'm confused. "I don't play, sir."

Now my face reddens as all at the table laugh at my expense. The Lord stops them with palms extended. "Jake was raised on the plains, and in Oregon, far from our vineyards and even farther from France." He turns to me, and in his scholarly manner, advises, "Champagne is served in tall, thin glasses called flutes, nothing to do with the instrument."

I clear my throat, and speak my mind. "If it's not an insult, sir, I'd as soon have a beer to quench my thirst."

Not to be outdone, he instructs the waiter, "Bring young Jake a flute and serve him the bubbly as well as a beer to quench his thirst." Then to me, "You must broaden your horizons, young man. My blessed wife made me promise to make a gentleman of you."

So, I raise my flute, "To Mrs. Stanley-Smyth, a lady without peer." And we all toast. And I feel much less stupid.

The rest of them are into their entrées, which appear to be roasted bird of some kind. I'm hungry, and although I've only partaken of raw shellfish once, don't hesitate. I quickly decide they're better with a squeeze of lemon and don't hesitate to finish them off; with the last swallow the plate is whisked away and replaced with a bowl of what the waiter mutters is consommé. The oysters had a red powder sprinkled over them, so I interrupt the Lord to inquire, "Sir, the red powder?"

"Paprika, all the way from Austria-Hungary."

"Thank you."

Lord Stanley-Smyth had long ago chastised me for not asking about things I knew little of, so I've never hesitated since and he's always quickly responded without derision.

Consommé, I quickly discover, is a clear soup with the flavor of beef, with a sprig of greenery floating on its surface. It, too, seemed to be blessed with a squeeze of the yellow tart fruit and a sprinkle of what the Lord advised was paprika.

I've yet to say hardly a word as my three companions have chatted without addressing me, until the soup bowl is whisked away and my roasted-to-a-rich-brown bird delivered.

This time the waiter doesn't inform me, so I turn to the Lord. "And this is?"

"Squab, pigeons before the muscle toughens up with flight."

I take a quarter of the breast and give him an

approving nod, getting a chuckle in return. He adds, under his breath, "The portions are small. You can eat again at the hotel." And chuckles again.

"I'm enjoying the experience," I say, and don't mention the sausage man and his cart normally near the entrance of the Niantic. I wouldn't think of insulting my host.

Tennessee Tom has finished and dabs his mouth with the cloth napkin each of us has at our plate side. He clears his throat, and asks, "So, does this recently departed have any kin or associations here in the city?"

It's obvious he's a cautious man.

The Lord turns to me. "You seem to have contacts the others of us would have little to do with...common sailors and their environs and such. After your morning deposition, how about sticking your nose into the cracks and crannies of the city and finding an answer for Tom?"

"Yes, sir. If there's any scuttlebutt, I'll ferret it out. And with your permission, send Barnabas on the same mission."

"A sound idea, now, I've ordered us each a soufflé made with vanilla bean imported from Mexico."

I have no idea what a soufflé might be, and even less a vanilla bean. The rest of them are silent but I can't help but ask, "Vanilla beans?"

He gives me a pleasant smile, as if glad I asked and pleased to show his knowledge.

"The delicious vanilla bean has its origins deep in the jungles, the south of Mexico. It was a well-kept—a threat of death if exposed—secret by the indigenous Totonac Indians for centuries. The Totonac Indians, later conquered by the Aztecs, kept these delicious vanilla plants to themselves. It was only when the Aztec Empire fell to Hernán Cortés, a Spanish conquistador, that vanilla was shipped back to Spain in the sixteenth century. And even later was vanilla introduced to Europe and then, of course, to the rest of the world. It made almost a full circle, coming back to us here in Alta California."

Miss Alice raises her glass of what I presume is champagne. "To the Totonacs." And we toast again.

Tom, not to be outdone, raises his flute again. "And to the hope this hooligan I was forced to send to hell...the hope he has no relatives or associates mislead enough to think he should be revenged."

We all drink to that, but without another word.

5

MY MA'S A GREAT COOK, CAN DO A BISCUIT THAT'LL DANG near float off the plate, yet crunch like a cracker. But so long as she's not in hearin' distance, I gotta sing the praises of that thing they called a soufflé, hitting the table hot, brown as a filly's eyes, yet light as a whiffy spring cloud, smelling good enough to make your chops water and you lick your lips until raw, and is as near to heaven as anything to eat can be. Particularly when topped with a concoction of sweet white cream kissed with a hint of brandy. Even though still a little hungry, I didn't stop at the sausage street vendor...I didn't want to get the taste of that heavenly soufflé off my tongue.

I dreamed of it.

As usual I was up before the cock crowed, did a quick washcloth bath with the cold water in the white crockery pitcher and bowl, brushed the dirt off my twill trousers and flannel shirt, spit shined my brogans, and headed for the Kingdom Freight and Mail Company and my good friend Barnabas. I didn't want to look too prosperous to the coppers as rumors fly of most of them being more than willing to extend a hand...a handout palm up.

Barnabas was grooming mules when I entered, and didn't stop, only yelling "Howdy, knee buster," over his shoulder as he continued with a currycomb.

"I promised some biscuits and gravy," I said, to his back.

"You promised breakfast. When I'm into your fat purse, steak and cackleberries seems more to my liking."

I have to laugh. "Since I'm still in your debt, steak and eggs it is. Kick the mule dung off'n your boots as we're headed from breakfast to the marshal's office to deliver a statement on last evening's events."

"The Purple Parrot is twixt here and there, and they serve a fat beefsteak...maybe beef is only a guess, probably horse or burro but fat, alongside a pile of fried spuds topped with two *huevos*, cooked as you like 'em."

"Then we're off," I say. I sailed with Spaniards, Mexicans, and Peruvians, and know enough of their language to know *huevos* are eggs. Fact is I can say restaurant, bathroom, thank you, excuse me, good morning, in a half-dozen languages...but am hardly fluent in any, my ma would say English among those in which I'm lacking.

The breakfast is all it's rumored to be. And the Purple Parrot is confident with a sign over the counter saying "Complain and you won't be charged, but you'll wear it. Our fine cook is a pugilist as well." But the fact is there's nothing to complain about, in fact we send, via the waitress, our compliments to the pugilist and compliment our waitress with a generous two-bit tip.

The marshal's office is only two blocks from the restaurant, and we're perched on the board steps when the door is unlocked at eight a.m. Of course, the copper behind the desk informs us that the marshal or the two coppers involved, Sergeant Zeb O'Madden and Patrol Officer Alex O'Toole aren't expected until after ten as they're investigating a homicide down in the Tenderloin. I extend my hand to the desk officer. "Jake Zane, here to give a statement."

He shakes with a tight smile. "Officer Ferral McPeters."

I notice there's a tiny restaurant next to the marshal's office, the Copper Kettle, so I ask, "Have you partaken of your coffee this morning, Officer McPeters?"

"Had a cuppa when the sun came up. Why?"

"Headed next door to wait for the marshal's return. Can I fetch you a cup?"

"Never turned down a free cup, kind of you."

"A selfish act, sir. I'm happy to be of service to them who protect us."

He nods, looking a little suspicious, but nods.

As we exit the door, Barnabas gives a little chuckle. "You are some kinda synco...what's the word, dictionary worm?"

"I would imagine you're looking for sycophant. My old daddy taught me a few things, and one I've found helpful is it's nice to have powerful, influential friends, but just as nice, sometimes more so, to have friends in low places. They ofttimes gain you audience with them more powerful...or warn you of their plans."

"Your daddy seems a wise soul."

"He was."

As we enter the Copper Kettle—I wonder if it's named to attract the building full of coppers next door—Barnabas spots a hand-written sign, *Dried apricot pie, a thin dime a slice*.

"Hows about them apples...or should I say apricots? You forgot to buy dessert with that breakfast."

I laugh. "I'm good for the nickel for coffee and another dime for pie, then you're on your own." Then I add, "I hope the cook can make pies better than he can spell."

We're no more than settled, yet to get our coffee, when two big, ugly blokes enter and take a table next to us. One, with a big, round head, double or more chin, one ear bit in half, and hardly enough hair to keep him from sunburn...in fact his cheeks and pate are speckled with brown sunspots. His eyes flare when he catches my gaze. He doesn't rise, but his voice raises as porky speaks to his mate.

"Lookee there, Ian, if that ain't that Jake Zane, I'll eat my hat. That bounty still good?"

6

THE OTHER WALLABY, I'D GUESS THEM TO BE, AS TALL AS his mate but thin as one of the establishment's doors and lacking no hair, shrugs as he turns to eye me. His Adam's apple bounces as he speaks.

"Damn if it ain't, lessen he's got a twin."

I don't wait but speak up. "I'm Jack Zane. You're thinking of my cousin, Jake. We look alike but of course I'm much more fetching." I remove my hat and lower my eyes, pouting a bottom lip before I moan, "Poor Jake, he was drowned off the Sandwich Islands. He wasn't worth a hoot in the shrouds. Fell from sixty feet up."

Porky isn't buying it. "A man shouldn't lie like that, mate."

"And a man would be a fool to start trouble next to a building full of coppers."

He guffaws, then settles, and growls, "You got me there, mate, but I got you when you distance yourself from them fat coppers. Now let me be while I fill up on bangers and mash."

I turn to Barnabas. "Dang if a bucket of lard ain't calling others fat."

Barnabas has turned to face them, his hand resting on his Colt. He waits until the waitress gets the big Wallabys attention, then turns back to me. "Trouble?"

I nod. "Left over from the affair with the knee. I was hoping it long forgotten. Word will be all over the city that I'm here…but it matters little as it likely would have nonetheless."

Barnabas smiles, and says low so they can't hear, "You want me to pick a little more serious row with these louts so we can end this right here? I checked my loads before we left the barn."

"You're too good a friend, old friend. Let's settle the Tennessee Tom matter before we have to explain putting a couple of Sydney Ducks in the ground, should we be quicker."

"Your lips to God's ears, if God listens to such plans," Barnabas says, but he moves around to sit at my left so his back's not to the threat.

Slim has biscuits and gravy and porky near the same, only the sausage and gravy is ladled over a six-inch-high pile of fried potatoes. Even so, shoveling it in like the place was on fire, they finish before we're halfway through our pie. We're not hurrying as we're topping off that fat steak. They rise and the big one steps over and leans on his knuckles on our table. He zeros his pig eyes on me.

"You know, bloke, you won't be so lucky next time. Were I you, I'd go to carving my stone."

I give him my best smile, which I turn to a snarl. "After I sharpen my chisel on your backbone, if'n I can get through all that fat. You saving that gravy in your mustache for lunch?"

"Bugger you," he snarls, but wipes his mouth with the back of a ham-sized hand.

His partner is up and heading for the door, and yells over his shoulder, "Otto, there's coppers on their way. There'll be another day."

And porky, who I now know as Otto, waddles after him.

Dang if it ain't Sergeant Zeb O'Madden and Patrol Officer Alex O'Toole, likely my two best nonpaying customers at The Piccadilly.

"Join us," I invite as they enter. And they do. "I hear y'all were on a homicide this morning?"

Zeb replies, "Aye, but first was that Otto Prager I saw leaving?"

"Overheard his mate call him Otto, so I'd guess so."

Zeb shakes his head. "He's the worst sort, boss says… and I shouldn't say it…but the boss says any legal excuse, we should blow holes in the worthless scum."

"And his mate?" I ask.

"Pauly Poundstone, another Wallaby. Don't let either of them behind you.

"Nothing much new," Zeb says. "Some whore got herself sliced from her personal up to her Adam's apple. Whore, but a good looker."

"Did y'all catch the coward?" I ask.

"Not the foggiest. She was up in the woods near the fort, some boot prints, but that's it."

"A pity," I say, and mean it. No one deserves to die like that unless they've done it to others.

"Ain't the first one. We've had five before her die the same way. Same low-life killer we think. Seems he don't want to pay for their services."

I rub my chin, then offer, "I'd guess it's something more than that. This fella is touched in the head.

Makes me wonder, these women still have their knickers on?"

"Come to think of it, they did," Alex says, seemingly in thought.

"Then, I'd guess, it wasn't the cost of their services got them gutted. Maybe this crazy man takes umbrage at their profession? Any ladies killed that weren't soiled doves?"

Zeb replies, "We had one female killed a couple of weeks ago, but she was shot dead by her husband. Seems she was dallying with the neighbor."

"I'd be looking for a crazy man, maybe one who claims to be pious." And I laugh. "One who might even preach his twisted religion but doesn't give Mary Magdalene her due."

Neither of the coppers reply, but both seem in thought, so I add, "How about I buy y'all some breakfast?" The Lord insisted I gain as many "owe-mes" as I can from the coppers and judges.

And they jump to.

After they've ordered, I ask, "Has the marshal returned?"

They both nod, so we excuse ourselves, getting a worried look as if I forgot saying I'd buy. I stop by the waitress, pay their tab, and get a cup of coffee in a big mug to take to the desk officer, having to leave an outrageous two-bit deposit on a crockery cup not worth a thin dime.

As we head over to the marshal, I spot Otto and slim across the street, sucking on stogies, eyeballing us. I give them a wave and am not surprised that my politeness is not returned.

The desk cop, Ferral McPeters, seems surprised when I hand over the mug. He nods and thanks me, and hustles away to inform the marshal we've appeared. I'm not a bit surprised to be told to take a seat. I've found, dealing with folks, ship captains in particular, that being made to wait seems a way of them letting one know how important they are. So Barnabas and I put our backsides on a hard bench and trade tales for twenty minutes until we're summoned.

The marshal has a young man at a nearby small desk record our statements, ink on parchment, and has us sign. Barnabas, which doesn't surprise me, makes his X as it seems he was raised where there was no school.

As we exit, Tennessee Tom is entering, Miss Alice in tow.

"All's well?" he asks, without so much as a good morning.

"Told it like it was," I say, giving them both a doff of my hat.

"See you back at the shop," Miss Alice says, then adds, "A new associate is there. Colt Barberosa. He'll be our roving gun. Good man to have looking out for us. Good man for you to treat like a brother and have about you like you're one of his."

I answer with a "Yes, ma'am." I'm still a little tongue-tied around this beautiful woman.

As we reach the bottom of the entry stairs, I note that Otto and slim are still across the street, and as we stride out stay a block behind. I don't like being dogged, but better to solve the problem on our own back forty. So long as they don't close the distance, all they'll get from me is being watched closely.

Seems they have that five-hundred-dollar reward in mind.

They'll get either that, or an ounce of lead for the trying.

7

AFTER ONLY A BLOCK WE CROSS A STREET BRIMMING WITH drays, horsebackers, a beer wagon pulled by a four-up of gray-dappled farm horses, a squad of marching dragoons, and one coach nearly as fancy as the Lord's. On the far corner, coppers Zeb and Alex stand observing it all, Zeb swinging his nightstick anchored to one finger.

As we near, I ask, "Trust you enjoyed your breakfast."

Zeb answers, "Did…obliged."

I decide having my rear guarded would not be a bad idea so invite them. "Have you seen the work on the new Piccadilly?"

"Just from the boardwalk," he replies.

"How about letting me show off a little. Come take a gander?"

"Fact is it's our duty to know the layout of all the primary buildings. This is as good a time as any." He gives me a nod and slips the nightstick into its loop on his belt. I glance over my shoulder as we stride off, Otto and slim are on the far corner, looking a little disappointed.

It's near six blocks to the Pick and we make it without breaking stride. Walk with a couple of coppers and all give way to your progress, even those mounted or with reins in hand aboard wagons and buggies.

The place is buzzing with workmen finishing the elaborate bar, staining the tables and chairs, unrolling Chinese carpets on the balcony above, and hauling others into the bordello. Perched on one of the few captain's chairs in a corner is a fella who would be handsome were it not for a scar from mid on his left ear to his chin. He rises when we enter and strides over.

"You the Zane kid?" he asks.

"I'm Jake Zane." I'm pretty sure who he is as he sports two nickeled revolvers, the one on his left butt forward.

"Colt Barberosa," he says, extending a hand.

Zeb puts on his copper face, standing with hands on hips. "*The* Colt Barberosa, recently from San Diego?"

"My business, not yours," Barberosa says, almost curling his lip at the two officers.

"I thought they was gonna hang you?"

Barberosa is silent for a moment, then almost spits it out. "Pretty damn sure they gotta find you guilty before you face the thirteen turns, and that jury said I was far too pretty to hang. Unless the law works crossways here in Frisco, they'd find the same."

"Law works fine," Zeb snapped. "Should one abide by it. I'd surely remember that, Barberosa."

"Got me a fine job right here, keeping the peace in this little bit of paradise, Officer," he replies, saying "officer" with obvious derision. They nod at each other.

"We'll talk later," I say, stepping in between them. Barberosa gives us his back without another word, and heads for the captain's chair, and I continue my tour, sorry that didn't go better as I'll need them both on my side. We take a leisurely tour and just as we return to the batwings, Tennessee Tom and Miss Alice are entering.

"Go well?" I ask.

"Well as can be expected," Tom replies, then sees Colt Barberosa over in the corner and strides over, extending a hand. They greet as if long-lost brothers.

"Old friends," Miss Alice says. "And these gentlemen are?" She gives Zeb and Alex one of those devastating smiles and extends a hand. Before I can speak, Zeb introduces himself. Alex ignores the hand and not only doesn't return the smile, but rudely turns away.

So Alice drops the hand and merely nods, and says, "I hope we see you here often, gentlemen," then excuses herself and ascends the stairs.

Both of them watch her silently all the way to the landing above.

Finally, Zeb mutters, "I truly hope she's working next door."

I laugh, then reply, "Only as management, as I understand it. Then, I don't know what's on the menu next door. All new to me."

They thank me for the tour. One of the men hired as a bartender is stacking bottles behind the bar, so I advise Zeb and Alex to wait a moment and stroll over and grab two bottles of what I know to be our cheaper whiskey, Black Widow, and return and hand one to each of them. "I appreciate your time."

"Don't suppose you got a sack," Zeb says. "Won't do to wander the streets with 'em."

I laugh. "How about I hang on to them and you drop by when off duty."

"Good'o," he says.

As they push through the doors, I catch a glance of Otto and slim across the street, and now they've been joined by two others, obviously cohorts.

"Hold up," I ask Zeb and Alex, and wave Tom and Colt over.

I address Zeb. "Do you mind if we solve a problem with the Wallabys right now?"

"Mind?" Zeb says. "You can wipe the road with them, and I'll shout your praises."

So I turn to Tom and Colt. "Time to go to work, gentlemen. You see those four across the way, eyeing the place and suckin' on those stogies?"

Both Tom and Colt eyeball the four, looking over the top of the batwings.

I add, "They want to take my head to their boss. I'd like to discourage them and now is as good a time as any."

"Give us time to get situated," Tom says, then he and Colt confide then both leave, Tom turning one way outside and Colt the other.

I have my revolver on my hip but prefer not to have a gun battle in front of the Piccadilly, but I have a quart of whiskey in both hands and decide that will likely do. I wait until Tom and Colt have both walked to opposite ends of the block and crossed. When I see them each about fifty feet from the four, I push through the batwings and stride across the road, dodging a wagon loaded with lumber. Otto, the biggest of the four, had pointed me out to the rest the moment I exited.

As I near they all have eyes on me, and hands on the revolvers at their sides...but I'm walking their way with bottles, maybe gifts, in hand. I believe they're confused.

I'M A LITTLE MORE THAN AN ARM'S LENGTH FROM BIG Otto and see Tom and Colt flanking the four, so I yell, "Hey, Tom," looking his way. All four of the Wallabys follow my glance, and big Otto turns back to me just in time to get a very close look, then a taste, of Black Widow as the bottle smashes into his forehead and blood sprays, the other three turn their attention to me, away from Tom and Colt…a mistake, as two of them go down like dropped sacks of rocks with heavy revolvers up aside their heads. The fourth one is trying to draw his sidearm but Colt has his revolver jammed under his chin so quickly it was a blur to me.

Otto has only gone to his knees, but his eyes are swimming. I'm deciding if I need to bust the other bottle on his pate when the quandary is solved. Tennessee Tom hits him so hard with his revolver, I'll be surprised if he ever awakens.

With all four of the Wallabys on the boardwalk—Colt has disarmed the fourth and forced him to his belly—Zeb and Alex trot up.

Zeb slides to a stop, shaking his head. "These no-accounts attacked you, gentlemen. We saw it all."

Before we can agree, they have loosened handcuffs from their belts and have the Wallabys cuffed to each other, still on the ground. Another copper trots up and stops, a little confused, and asks Zeb, "You sure you're cuffin' the right bunch, I saw—"

Zeb cuts him off. "You saw these filthy Ducks attack our good friends. Friends helpin' rid the streets of these scum. These four are going to the lockup. Had I my way, they'd be going to hell."

The new officer sputters a minute, then pulls his cuffs out of his belt and hands them to Zeb. "I don't believe that big fella is going to walk anywhere for a while. I'll run fetch the meat wagon."

"Good man," Zeb says.

"Owe you," I say, and slap Zeb on the back. "Thanks for the loan of your bottle. Hope to see you later?"

"You bet."

As the three of us are crossing the road back to The Piccadilly, Colt has a belly laugh. "Damned if it ain't okay to have the law on your side…leastways one time in life."

"Let's keep it that way," I caution as I push through the batwings.

Taking Miss Alice's advice, as Tennessee Tom wanders off to make sure the painting of the layout of the faro tables is correct, I invite Colt Barberosa to sit and jaw a minute. I see he's a man of action and just hope that action will be in The Piccadilly's favor. Being harsh with customers, to my way of thinking, is not always in the house's favor. Killing them, unless for very good reason, is never so. That said, all I can do is advise and I've learned advising older, far more mature folks is an exercise in gentle tact. And particularly when advising someone who can put the muzzle of his revolver under your nose so fast it's a blur.

My ma would call Mr. Barberosa taciturn. I have to work hard to get much more than a yes or no from him.

"So, where do you hail from, Colt. May I call you by your given—"

"Yep."

He's also not much for teasing as when I ask, with a smile, "You're from yep?" He's not amused.

"East," he replies.

"Lots of country out east. And too many states now for me to start guessing."

"Don't matter."

"No, sir, I guess it doesn't. You seem handy with that sidearm. Were you a law officer, or dragoon?"

"Nope."

I have to chuckle. "You're not long on chatter…"

"Nope. Never felt the need."

"I hear you let your sidearm do the talking."

"Only when necessary. Never kilt no one didn't need the killing."

"Well, sir, I'd guess that a good thing, particularly when we want our customers at the tables losing their money, or at the bar bending an elbow, not pushing up daisies."

"Or next door with the sportin' ladies."

"True enough. You understand I'm not your boss. I'm only here as Lord Stanley-Smyth's eyes."

"Yep. And that gentleman tolt me to make sure you stayed seein'…stayed alive."

"Your efforts in that regard would certainly be appreciated by my ma, my sisters, and myself. Along that line, I thank you for discouraging those Wallabys."

"My pleasure. I'm fairly sure that affair is yet to end."

"A good observation."

"Yep," he says, and we end the conversation without me knowing much more about Colt Barberosa than I did when we sat down.

I glance up to see a man standing in the doorway, each of the batwings resting on one side and the other, so he fills the doorway. He was, at first glance, dressed like a bum with a loose-fitting robe to his knees, hair to the center of his back, Jesus sandals, and the floppy brimmed hat of a wayfarer. His scraggly beard falls to midchest. I stand eying him for a moment, hoping he'll wander away, but he doesn't so I wandered over, Colt behind me.

"May I help you, sir?" I ask.

"Are you the proprietor?" he replies, his voice raspy but with a certain authority.

"I'm his representative. May I help you?"

"I had a dire fear this work would only continue the foul purpose of this den of inequity."

"This is merely a saloon, my friend, with a few games of chance."

"Money changers," he mumbles. "Then wicked Jezebels are no longer employed here?"

His shifty, watery eyes continue to rove over the place, and have not once centered upon mine.

"We have no women in the employ of The Piccadilly." It's not a lie, even though I intend to employ at least two attractive barmaids, to whet the appetite of the customers who'll wander next door to have that appetite sated.

"I have seen them entering and leaving. Hell will welcome a man who lies to a man of the cloth."

"Women have access to an establishment next door. But are not employed here. It's nice to meet you, Pastor or Preacher or however you'd like to be addressed, but I have work so please excuse us."

"You may address me as Elohim. I will retire now… but I will be watching…and I'm all-seeing."

That takes me back a little, but not for long. "I hope you enjoy watching our progress. We'll be open in less than a fortnight."

With that he spins on a sandaled heel and strides away, his sandals flopping, his robe billowing behind.

"Elohim?" Colt asks from over my shoulder.

"Yep, I'd guess his mother didn't give him that name."

"How so?"

"It's another word for God. If he gave it to himself, he holds himself in pretty dang high regard."

"Maybe, but he smelt like a goat."

Again I have to chuckle. "One of my ma's favorite quotes from the Good Book, 'Why do you look at the speck of sawdust in your brother's eye and pay no attention to the plank in your own eye?'"

He looks puzzled. "What the hell does sawdust have to do with things?"

I laugh. Gunfighter, yes; philosopher, no. So I get back to smells. "Maybe he is half goat; he had a billy goat beard."

"Let's hope he keeps ploddin' along."

"I'll second that, but I dang sure doubt it. And don't doubt he'll be a nuisance."

"Let's hope nuisance is the worst of it."

9

THE REST OF THE WEEK IS UNEVENTFUL, AND WE DECIDE to open on Monday. Things are pretty well in order. Miss Alice has eight ladies eager to see if the high price of two dollars a poke works, of course they have the option of negotiating for more, sometimes receiving much more. All the ladies have been examined by Dr. Southerby, a former Missouri man with whom I've struck up a friendship, and found clean and healthy. Tennessee Tom has hired three bartenders and four dealers, a Dutch couple, Lars and Emma de Jong, who'll cook the light fare offered, and a swamper, Abe, a former slave who uses only that given name...who I've also taken to.

I came west with Sampson, an escaped mute slave, his tongue cut out by a heinous plantation overseer. He became my best friend during that long journey, a co-protector of my ma and sisters after my pa passed. To be truthful, I couldn't have done it, the near two-thousand-mile trek, without him.

Abraham, our swamper, of course called Abe, is not

as massive a man as Sampson, but he's near my tall and barrel chested. He easily handled a fifty-gallon hog's head barrel of pickles—snatching it off the wagon and carrying it hugged to his chest—as we stocked the place. I praised him with a laugh and slap on the back and got a nod and near smile in return. No doubt that load over three hundred pounds and clumsy besides. I have no interest in wrestling him. I have no idea how he got to California but will ferret that out of him.

Like most Africans he's a quiet man. I guess had I and my people been subjugated and treated less than human for generations, and in a subservient position where we could be flogged or hung for speaking out, I'd learn to be reticent to speak. Sampson was mute but we learned to communicate, and I'll continue to assure Abe of my friendship and am sure he'll become more talkative. He looks to me to be a good man to have alongside.

As it's Sunday, the day before our quiet preopening—we plan to work the bugs out before a grand opening the following Saturday—I'm doing a walk-through of the facilities. I'm excluding the sportin' house side and have avoided having anything to do with it. My ma's recriminations haunt me even though she's near seven hundred miles away, as the crow flies.

Miss Alice is responsible for her side, and I'll let her be Lord Stanley-Smyth's eyes. Except when it's time to count the take.

My new friend, Officer Alex O'Toole enters, looking less than happy.

I stroll over to meet him. "Can I stand you to three fingers of decent whiskey?" And give him a wide smile.

"You've yet to hear?" he asks, his brow furrowed.

"Hear? Hear what?"

51

"Zeb was murdered in his bed in the night. His wife beside him. Both bludgeoned to death."

I'm dumbstruck for a moment, then I can feel the heat raise up my backbone. "Wallabys?" I ask.

"God only knows, but that's our first guess. That big fella, Otto, your man whacked with his revolver...well, he ain't right in the head anymore. Seems the Wallabys have their dander up. We're rounding them up now. The jail will be full if we get half of them. You best tell Mr. Barberosa to watch his back as I suspect he'll be next on their list."

"I'll tell him. I'll be happy to help with that interrogation. Me and my cat-o'-nine-tails."

"You've got a cat-o'-nine-tails?"

"No, but I'll make one or buy one on this occasion."

"We have a couple of copper blokes who'll not spare the rod to get some information. But those Ducks are a tough lot and know worse'll be done to 'em should they rat out their mates."

"That drink?"

"On duty, but this day don't mind if I do."

I know that Abe has taken a room in the Tenderloin, where many of the Wallabys hang out. He's polishing some tables, so I call him over as I'm pouring for Alex.

"Yes, sir," he sidles up to us at the bar.

"Abe, this is Officer Alex."

"Honored," Abe says, but doesn't extend a hand. I presume he's not used to doing so with white folks.

To Alex's credit, he does, and Abe shakes.

"Alex, Abe lives over in the Tenderloin. If you don't mind, I'll have him ask around," then turn to Abe, "You can do so safely? Don't want to get you killed."

"All them folks, working as maids and cleaners and stable hands an' such, hear what's going on. White folks talk like the darkies got no ears. I'll act like I like the gossip."

It's the longest speech I've heard from Abe.

Then he adds, speaking to Alex, "That suit you, Officer sir?"

"Obliged. We'll take all the help we can get. The whole force has Zeb's murder first on their plate. And always do when a fellow officer is killed."

"Then I go back to polishin'," Abe says, giving us a nod and his back.

After he leaves, I ask, "I overheard you two asking about each other's children. He leave behind some young'uns?"

"Six-year-old daughter, three-year-old son."

"How are they going to get by?"

"We got a small fund, but it won't last two months. She has folks over in Sacramento and will head there."

"The Piccadilly would like to add a twenty-dollar gold piece to that fund." And I go behind the bar and fish one out of the till. I'll leave a note and explanation there so the accounts balance.

Alex takes the coin and gives me a nod and sad smile. "Thanks, Jake. I'll let all on the force know your thoughtfulness."

"The Piccadilly's, please."

"Aye, The Piccadilly's."

Lord Stanley-Smyth has called a meeting for this evening, drinks and a ham and bean supper on the house for all. We're surprised to learn it's his final appearance for a good long while as he has business in New York and possibly London and we won't see him for months.

I'll be the only one signing on his establishment accounts. He's made clear to Miss Alice and Tennessee Tom that I'm there only as overseer and they have the final say on the operation of their individual areas—but the fact is I hold the purse strings. So, I wonder if they really think they're their only boss. They have to come to me for any improvements or expenditures. I once heard another interpretation of the Golden Rule, and that is the guy who has the gold makes the rules.

It's gonna be interesting how this plays out. Tomorrow at three p.m. the doors open, and to me, the fun—or the fury—begins.

Lord Stanley-Smyth wraps an arm around my shoulders as I'm walking him to the Niantic after our company supper.

He wishes me luck as he climbs the stairs.

I won't see him again for months.

10

I GUESS I SHOULD BE SURPRISED WHEN I UNLOCK THE inner doors on Monday, promptly at three, and swing the batwings aside to wave waiting customers in. I'm not surprised as we've been advertising "first drink free." The waving sign just outside the door figuratively hits me in the face, at least three feet wide by five tall, held by the man in the robe and sandals, frizzy hair to his waist, who calls himself God, or Elohim. He's loudly chastising the crowd, which gets the hair up on the back of my neck.

I stride forward, he's facing away, reach over his shoulder and grab the sign at the same time I give him a shove off the boardwalk and into the muddy street. Unfortunately, his sandals stick in the mud and he goes face first into the muck and horse apples.

Now I'm embarrassed, but haven't lost my sense of capitalism, so before I go to help him up, yell to the townsmen, drovers, and mariners, "Sorry, fellas. Go on in, first drink is on me. Enjoy San Francisco's finest saloon and gambling house."

Only then do I step out into the mud and help the robed man to his feet. The sign is lettered, both front and back.

REPENT YOU SINNERS, YOU DEBAUCHERS, YOU MONEY CHANGERS. HELL AWAITS.

As I pull him to his feet, I ask, "I'm not calling you Elohim, friend. I've only got one God."

"And you'll never meet him," he sputters. "You'd be one of those who drove the nails through His holy bones."

"No, sir. I would not. But I'll not have you—"

"This is a public street. I'm allowed…"

I don't challenge his statement as he's likely right. I was a little overaggressive, so now a little embarrassed. If he's truly a man of the cloth, I'm ashamed.

"You're right, sir. But you're not allowed to block the entry. March and wave your sign to your heart's content. Just don't block the entry." I hand him two bits. "This will cover the cost of laundering your robe."

"You'll burn in hell, along with your Jezebels."

"Not for a while, I hope. Plop down on the bench over there and I'll have someone bring you out a bowl of beans and chunk of hard bread. On the house today."

"I'll not take sustenance from the hands of heathens."

I shrug, decide it best to just let him be, and spin on my heel and head back to my work.

As instructed by Lord Stanley-Smyth, I climb the stairs and take my place on the quarter round of the front of the balcony, where I can oversee most the tables and bar. I'm pleased to note all but two barstools are occupied, and this one minute after a cold opening, and as we only have four dealers on hand all twenty-four of their seats are taken, and players stand behind betting, and drinking.

Looks like a good deal of the town is curious about The Piccadilly.

Nearly every afternoon of the past week Tennessee Tom has given me instructions on the games, particularly faro, the primary game on the gambling floor, so I'm well versed. Two decks are used, thirteen squares painted on the table each for a number, ace through king. Players bet on a number, when all bets are taken the dealer turns over two cards. The first is a loser and the house takes the bet, say the player bet on a three and the first card turned is a three. The dealer picks up that bet and wins. The second card turned, is a jack. The dealer pays any bet on the jack. If two jacks are turned by the dealer, then he takes half the bet on the jack.

He's also instructed me on the myriad ways players, and dealers, cheat. Particularly the hardest form which is when dealers are in cahoots with a player.

All four of our hired dealers are men of experience. All four have dealt on riverboats, one in New Orleans as well, and one in New York. They are fast and experienced, but I catch one. He has a silver coin, polished flat on a side, so flat it is reflective. He places it on the table so seat six, immediately to his right, can see a reflection of the bottom card if he holds the deck just so. Then the dealer, with a fairly easy motion, moves the bottom card to the second card to be dealt. That is the winning number. I noticed as Tom had instructed me to watch for a player who bet low, maybe two bits, and lost, but every three or four hands would bet high, in this instance two dollars and win. It took me an hour watching, but I finally get on to it.

I shout down to Tom, who is cruising the tables and encouraging the players, and he comes up.

"You got a bottom switch on table four, seat six is his partner."

"You're positive. He's been winning and losing."

"Winning big bets, losing small. Just as you told me to watch for."

"How's the dealer signaling the number?"

"Doesn't have to. He's showing him. He's got something reflective and lifting the deck so player six can see the bottom card before he does the switch. If you're on that side of the room, the player never bets more than a quarter. They're skinning us for a buck every three or four hands if you're on the other side of the room."

"I'll watch for a minute and brace them if I catch them," and he spins and heads for the stairway.

I get a bad feeling, either he didn't believe me, thought I was incompetent, or maybe stupid. What I thought was he should have caught them as he was on the floor and often closer to the cheats than I was. I didn't like my gut feeling.

Later, just before closing, I brace Tom. "I didn't see you bringing those cheats to Jesus."

"They quit playing before I could catch them. If they were cheating they've moved on now."

"Your dealer hasn't?"

He cuts his eyes away, then mutters. "Quinlon? He's a good man, known him a long time. I'll watch him close from now on."

I think it but don't say it. Known him a long time doesn't make me more comfortable. In fact, makes me less so.

We'll stay open so long as we have enough paying customers to double our cost, and this night we still have a full house at midnight. I've watched closely as a half-dozen customers have tried to take advantage of the free drink. We have two bartenders working so they approach the second to try and hustle another free one. But I catch several of them, yell down to the bartender, and he informs them they'll get the boot if they try again.

We have no real trouble until a big fella, my height but twice my weight, starts up the stairs and he's bouncing from railing to wall. Luckily Colt, who's stayed near the front door to ward off obvious bums only looking for the free goobers, sees the big drunk and hits the bottom of the stairway before the drunk reaches the top.

I meet him before he's halfway across the balcony, heading for the brothel door.

"Privies are out back, pardner," I admonish him.

It takes him a second to focus on me, then he roars, "I ain't your partner. I'm Bull Macklin, fresh off the...the...the fine...the fine German ship *Hamburg*. Clear the way ye sogger."

"Can't, friend. Come back when you haven't soaked your brain with our good sauce."

I'm glad to see Colt is only an arm's length behind the big man, and Abe has seen what was transpiring and at the top of the stairs.

"Won't do you any good to visit the ladies, friend. They have strict instructions to refuse service to a man in his cups as deep as you seem to be. Turn around and down the stairs. The next one is on me."

"Don't want no...no next...next one. Want me a poke. Been at sea more'n two months. Need me a...a poke from a fat whore."

"Sorry to say, we got nothing but skinny girls."

"Then skinny it be," he says, and pushes me aside.

59

Before he takes two steps Colt is on him and hits him hard behind a knee with his revolver, a move I've never seen. The big man folds and goes to his side then rolls to his back. Colt is bending over him. "You're mighty drunk, friend. You fell down."

"Little drunk, I...I guess," he mumbles. Then he seems to think a moment. Then he snarls at Colt. "You done hit me. Hit...me behind...from behind."

He starts to rise, but Abe steps up and sits on the man's chest. "You down, you stay down, afore my friend and I have to keep y'all down," he says, and the man who called himself Bull looks even more confused.

Finally, he manages, "You're a-sittin' on me."

"Yes, sir," Abe says, and bounces a little.

Bull turns green, and his eyes roll a little.

"Hold it," I yell, then add, "don't want him up'chuckin' on that new rug."

It's quiet for a moment, as we're in suspense as to what's about to soil the carpet, when Bull finally says, "You...you gots...you gots a room I can rent?"

"These fellas will help you down the stairs and out front and point you to the Highlander. Three to a bed only a quarter. Just a half block down and across the road."

I instruct them, "Make sure he makes it. The *Hamburg* has a crew of over fifty. Let's stay friendly with them."

When Colt and Abe return, I congratulate them on a job well done.

But I'm thinking, what a hell of a way to make a living.

11

THE NEXT FEW DAYS ARE UNEVENTFUL, AND WE'VE SET UP sort of a ritual, having coffee for Tennessee Tom and me, and English tea for Miss Alice each morning just before we open at nine. My little round table in my quarter round looking down on the tables fits us just fine. We discuss any problems encountered and I'm pleased they seek my council. I guess I shouldn't be too complimented as that likely comes from holding the purse strings.

I've also been introduced to the eight ladies working in the brothel—which includes a mother and daughter, Chinese, who run the baths and massage and are not available for other services. The eight all use nom de plumes, names they think will attract business. There's Marigold, called Goldy of course; Melinda; Daisy; Mary Magdalene, I presume who thinks she'll attract wayward Christians; Ruth of Sharon, who for some reason has the nickname Peaches, I have no idea where Sharon might be; Juliet, who I'm sure calls each of her customers

Romeo; Lily, one of the two Chinese girls; and Jade, another Chinese, and Lily's daughter.

We now have thirteen ladies employed, as Tom has hired two barmaids whose duties do not included those of the soiled doves next door. One is called Kansas, for obvious reasons, the other Morela. Both are clean and attractive and dress modestly, buttons up to their necks, not like the dance hall girls of other establishments. Morela is a buxom lass with a girth as wide as one of our captain's chairs. I'm a little surprised Tom put her to work as she has to move through our crowd balancing mugs of beers, then am more surprised to see how light on her feet she is. And she has a constant smile and seems honest, at least we've had no complaints about her making change.

They all seem nice and if met outside unbeknownst as to the soiled doves trade, would be found attractive and intelligent. I know each has their own story about how they wound up working a brothel, most because of circumstance, a few merely as it's the highest paid of the few jobs available to women in the West...or in the East for that matter.

It's the morning of our grand opening when I'm introduced to Elizabeth Portnoy, Miss Alice's niece. She, it seems, is foisted upon Alice as both Beth's parents died of cholera when only halfway between Chicago and San Francisco. The same ailment that took my father from us. I stand and am a little awestruck when Alice arrives with her at our morning coffee klatch.

"Jake," Alice says, with a bit of a coy smile, "my niece, Elizabeth, Beth to her friends and I'm sure you'll become one." It appears she's already met Tennessee Tom.

"She's not—" I start to question, shocked that Alice might bring a relative into the trade, particularly one so young and so beautiful. Not the classic beauty of her aunt, but a youthful beauty fresh as a Sunday morning in spring. Blond hair to her shoulders, eyes sparkling and blue as the deep Pacific over which I sailed for nearly two years, skin clear and clean as a flawless peeled apple.

"No," Alice interrupts. "However, she'll be with me in my quarters and will do odd jobs, likely in the kitchen if you approve, when not in school." Our kitchen is a small shack off the rear of the building, actually off both the brothel and the saloon so it can serve both. It's safer in case there's a fire which can hopefully be extinguished before spreading. On the brothel side is a woodbin, one hundred gallons of water and firehose; on the saloon side is a privy with two stalls serving the saloon, a fenced garbage area, and an access that leads into the kitchen shack, although a small hallway leading to the brothel.

I contemplate for a moment before replying to Miss Alice's request for her niece to work in the kitchen, wondering how safe it is. "Of course," I finally say, then ask, "Does she cipher and is her penmanship acceptable?"

Both she and Miss Alice laugh. "She's been in school since knee high."

"Then she can help me upon occasion, with the books, banking, and such."

"Wonderful, Beth lost her parents, my sister, to that damn cholera and she came on to California with a kind Mormon couple who brought her to me."

"So sorry, Miss Beth," I say.

"Thank you, Mr. Zane."

"Jake, please."

"Jake, and I'm Beth to my friends. And I hope you'll become one."

More than friends I hope, but don't say. "You're still in school?"

"I am. We'll be investigating nearby schools soon. I've been accepted at Mills Ladies in Benicia, founded just last year. I applied and was accepted before we left Chicago. But the new term is months away."

I haven't mentioned it to anyone else but feel the need to impress this young lady. I'd guess sixteen or seventeen tender years old. "I'm studying Latin and some...some mathematics, but on my own, mostly...on my own...in the morning before I report here."

"Really," she says, and flashes a smile for the first time. Miss Alice seems amused, I guess as I'm mumbling a bit. I don't know what Miss Alice has thought of me and my interests but has seemed surprised I haven't taken advantage of any of her ladies, even when offered as an "on the house" service. My uncle, famous for his philandering, died of the pox, and that cured me of any interest in ladies of the night. But I'm happy to have Miss Alice think I'm pious. And glad I have been as I'm sure Miss Beth would be offended, even though her aunt is a madam. As those ladies in charge of brothels are referred.

It should be a busy day for the grand opening. As it's Alex's day off, I hire him, requesting he wear his uniform. As much as I regret Zeb's demise—his killers yet to be found—I'm pleased to note Alex has received a promotion to sergeant, taking Zeb's position. We let him put a nice clean jug near the door with a sign, **Donations appreciated for fallen Officer Zeb O'Madden's children**.

As it turns out my spacious apartment, two rooms, with its four-foot-wide outdoor privy access and deck is in a prime location to look down upon the brothel's rear entrance, the one used by the town's prominent who don't want to be seen patronizing the place. Even so at night it's difficult to make out the face of those entering, and appropriately they have a red cast to their face from the coal oil lamp near the door, it with a red glass sconce. So they look devilish, and maybe are if customers of a house of ill repute. We work hard, however, to keep our ill repute reputation as healthy as possible. Already, open less than a week, I've seen a judge, the marshal, and two aldermen slip into the back door. And our girls all leave by that exit as they don't want to be followed, particularly by the drunks leaving the saloon. The ladies only leave to shop for their personals, or eat elsewhere which seems seldom, as they each have their own quarters and our cooks, Lars and Emma, keep beans and beef, chicken, or pork, and fresh bread at all times. He even has a generous supply of eggs and fried potatoes in the morning.

I have to laugh thinking of my position in life now as compared to aboard ship, when it was gruel with its generous occupation of weevils but lathered with molasses. I'm afraid I'm already spoiled rotten, eating now as good as I did on the farm with Ma's cooking.

Glancing at my recently acquired pocket watch, I see it's coming on nine and opening time. Again, we're offering free goober peanuts and a free beer. This time rather than try and remember who got the free drink, we're handing a wooden nickel to each as they enter. I'm sure some will sneak out and reenter, but so be it. It's a beer, not a whiskey.

Of course when I swing aside the batwings, there is the robed man who has the audacity to call himself Elohim, and he's blocking the doors with his five-foot sign.

This time I refrain from pushing him face first into

the muddy street. Rather, I sidle up to him. "Good morning. Please move down so folks have room to enter."

He puffs up like he's Moses on the mountain, and the spittle actually flies as he shouts, "I'll not give way so these wayward men can debauch themselves."

So I let free beer talk, and speak to the crowd. "Gentlemen, I'm going in for some free suds." And I turn and enter.

I'm not a bit surprised that the wave of men sweep Mr. Robe and his sign with them as they charge the opening. As soon as the crowd has softened to only two wide, I move to my nemesis, and ask, "Can I get you a beer, friend?"

"You can get me out of this harlot haven. Back to the road."

So, as requested, I lead him out. When back on the boardwalk, I suggest, "Please stay to the side so folks can enter. I have a copper on duty inside who'll be happy to escort you to the jailhouse should you restrict the flow of traffic. I believe it's called a misdemeanor nuisance."

"Humph," he says, so I nod and return to the saloon, and duck a thrown chair.

The place has erupted into a riot.

12

TWO DOZEN CUSTOMERS ARE AT IT HEAD AND HORN, tables overturned, chairs and stools flying. I imagine only moments before lead flies.

I've spoken a second too soon as a shot reverberates through the room and it suddenly goes dead silent, as dust motes drift down and the echo of the shot has all moving only their heads as they scan the room making sure they're not in the path of the next shot.

It's Colt Barberosa, standing on a chair, panning the crowd with a revolver in each hand. He shouts, in a tone that conveys there is no doubt he means every one of the few words. "Next man who swings gets a shoulder broke with a forty-four, unless I miss and you get one through the pumper."

Tennessee Tom has stayed out of the fray, and is leaning in a corner, eyeing all with interest but staying aloof. He has a hand on a pistol but has not pulled it.

Alex, to his credit, also climbs on a chair, and he's in uniform. "Next man swings on another will be the guest of the city, looking at the world through bars. My promise. Should he get himself shot I'll swear it was self-defense on Mr....."

It's quiet for a moment until one of four men flat on the floor moans.

I yell at Abe, who's been trying to separate fighters. "Mr. Abe, please get some rags for them that's bleeding, then gather up the broken furniture." Then I turn to the dealers. "You gentlemen running the games, try and get each player their chips back."

And that starts an uproar of arguments about who had how many chips in front of them and bet. So I yell again. "Take it outside if you want to continue to disagree. The disagreement, whatever it was, is over."

The grumbling has quieted. Only two separate pairs of combatants want to continue out in the street. Abe and I are happy to escort them out.

As we do I hear the ruckus raise ugly voices behind us and turn to see one of the combatants who was out cold and flat on his back, rising like Lazarus from the dead, and he's screaming, "That Ethiopian bastard knocked me cold, put his hands on me...he's gonna die."

The man has drawn his weapon and is panning the room, looking for the only African present, Abe, who he called an Ethiopian.

Abe, behind me, is about to step back inside. I spin and with a hand in his chest, and him looking surprised, give him a shove. "Stay out, some crazy lout is hunting for your handsome mug."

Abe gets it, and steps back.

Colt has dismounted the chair and behind the shouter, shoves the barrel of his revolver up against the back of the man's head. "Holster it, pilgrim. I don't want to have to clean your brains off'n the new lead ceiling."

He doesn't holster the weapon, rather drops it, and,

cocked, it fires and a nearby customer grabs his stomach and stumbles back, then falls, screaming, "I'm shot, damn, damn, damn…shot."

The shouter is standing with mouth hanging open, then he mutters, "Oh, mother of God. I didn't mean…I didn't shoot…it was an accident." He's looking around for a sympathetic face but sees none.

Apparently, the city-dressed fellow who's now blowing blood, probably with nearly his last breath, has friends with him, as two fellows fall on the shouter and begin pummeling him with their fists.

Now Alex jumps into the fray, swinging his night-stick to great effect, as Colt uses his revolver as a bludgeon, and they quickly have all three prostate and unconscious or nearly so.

Things seem settled, finally.

Only now do I notice Tom stepping away from leaning on the wall, now helping settle arguments about the distribution of chips. And the players seem to accept his word as final.

I take a deep calming breath, as the customers are righting tables and chairs, trying to allocate chips that have been spread all over the floor, some covered with the blood of combatants.

At the moment I'm feeling pretty dang smart for having Officer Alex on the job. His testimony will suffice, and my customers won't have to spend hours away from the tables giving statements.

He's standing near the now motionless dead fellow, awaiting other officers and the meat wagon to haul the body away. I'm a little astounded that others merely step around the corpse and go back to the bar or to the tables.

I have to shake my head and wonder what the hell I've gotten myself into, where you can get gutshot for merely standing and watching the excitement. Where others step around your body going cold as if you were a pile of cow poop in the road.

What a grand Grand Opening.

I retreat up the stairs to my perch overlooking all.

I guess the brawl and accidental shooting, if you can equate carelessness with accident, is enough excitement and by three o'clock the place is down to the dregs and not worth staying open, so I announce we're closing. The remaining are drunks and easily ushered out.

Unlike most establishments, who might hide their safe, our five foot tall by three foot wide by two foot deep Victor safe, trimmed in copper, is directly in the center of the gambling hall and saloon. It was my choice as should someone attempt to rob us, they'll be observed by all, if open. If they try to burgle during the short time we're closed, or take it away, they'd have to have ten pounds of black powder, awaking me and Abe, who occasionally sleeps in the cellar, and a dozen men to carry Victor away.

We are all exhausted from a very busy night and I have Colt escort Alice over from the brothel side with her take in a small canvas sack with her own lock, to which I have a key, and Tom gathers his cash and chips in a larger canvas bag, to which I have a key. We, together, lock them in the Victor. We'll do our count in the morning when fresh.

And it's a devil of a pile. I'm beginning to understand why Lord Stanley-Smyth was attracted to this heinous, I'm sure Godforsaken, business.

Even with Victor, I decide we'll bank daily, for as tough as our safe is, Adams and Company Express Office and Bank has one that would take ten pounds of black powder. And the rumor is there are two armed guards on hand during open hours, and one nearby at all times when closed.

Next to the city's banks and freight offices, I'd guess we'd be a grifter or robber's primary target.

Something to keep in mind.

13

IT'S A BEAUTIFUL MORNING, MADE EVEN MORE BEAUTIFUL as Beth arrives at my table at eight just after I've recovered the bags from Victor.

She flashes me a devastating smile. "Aunt Alice said you might want some help with the reconciliation and banking?"

"You're always welcome," I say.

Abe arrives with a pot of coffee and three cups, as it's usually Tom, Alice, and myself. So I ask Beth, "Do you take coffee?"

"I do, coffee or tea."

I pour her a cup and pass it and the little pitcher of cream he always has on the tray, and yell after him, "Mr. Abe, another cup when you have time."

"Mr. Tom has errands and said he'll not return until near noon, so's y'all have enough cups."

I push her the smaller brothel bag. "You count that one first and I'll count the Piccadilly bag, then we'll switch and check each other's numbers."

"I'll wager you a dime I don't miss a penny?" she challenges.

I laugh. "I'll pay you a dime you don't miss a penny, in addition to your wages of course. Is Miss Alice going to join us?"

"She has the sniffles and asked me if you'll forgive her?"

"Of course, I hope it's only the sniffles."

Beth gives me a tight smile. "My aunt is not only the most beautiful, but the strongest woman I've ever known."

"Well, Miss Beth, I don't know about your tough, but you'll run her a race for beautiful."

She cuts her eyes away, blushes red in the cheeks, and fans herself with a hand. "Thank you, but I don't fool myself. No one holds a candle to my aunt."

"I've said more than I should. Let's count."

The brothel has taken in over three hundred dollars, the saloon over two hundred—even with the free beers—and the tables another four hundred plus. The girls are paid daily, one half their take plus they receive room and board, paid before the take is turned over to me by Miss Alice. So the brothel take is nearly pure profit except for what little customers drink from the bar on that side, and the cost of what little food they might consume. The girls eat little and are limited to one drink per shift. I'll have to figure the cost of goods for the saloon and labor for the tables at the end of each week. But I'd guess the net profit is about equal for both sides. Lord Stanley-Smyth has probably cleared nearly five hundred dollars this single day.

Abe is down below swamping the floor, emptying spittoons, and refilling two big tubs of goobers. I yell down to him. "Mr. Abe, is Colt about?"

"No sir, it ain't nine yet."

"Do you have a sidearm?"

"Down under my mattress?"

"Fetch it. I'd like you to guard Miss Beth over to Adams Express to deposit the take that we don't need for change."

"Yes, sir," he says, and heads for the door and stairway leading down.

"Why, Mr. Jake Zane. You'd trust me with all that money. I might catch a ship to China."

"I can't imagine a thief thinking you'd be carrying all that money in a shopping bag, so trusting you is a selfish act. Bring me a receipt for the deposit, please."

"To the penny. I'll run and get one of Aunt Alice's shopping bags and my reticule."

As I watched her leave for Adams, Abe walking three feet behind as if he was an attentive slave—even as California is a free state some pass through with slaves—I'm having second thoughts. It's showing my trust and somewhat, admiration, of Beth, but it's also putting her at risk. To some, five hundred dollars is a king's ransom, and that's what she's carrying in gold and silver coin, a couple of gold slugs, and paper money.

Lord Stanley-Smyth spent two hours educating me on gold and silver coin, slugs—bars from one half ounce on up—and paper money. Customers hand all sorts of "money" to the bartender or to buy chips for the tables. Paper money printed by banks as far away as Boston, New York, and Philadelphia are shoved across the counter. As soon as we opened, our chips were accepted as payment by many nearby merchants, so in fact they were as good or better than most paper money. The farther away the bank, the more discount I insisted before accepting their paper. If East Coast paper, and I knew it not to be a failed bank, seventy-five percent was the discount. For a dollar, paper on a Boston bank you'd get a quarter's worth. Texas and Louisiana paper would get you fifty percent. And in both those cases our dealers and bartenders were taught to carefully inspect the paper as it had to be beautifully printed as counterfeiters worked hard at their craft. A ten-dollar banknote might be only worth its use in the privy.

Strangely, the gold flowing from the Sierras made the value of silver and copper increase. As Lord Stanley-Smyth explained the law of supply and demand, as gold, once rare, became more plentiful, other metals increased in value. And not only was gold discovered and mined and panned in California, but Australia has a boom as well. Gold has long been valued at sixteen dollars the ounce, and continues to be.

Mexican silver pieces, minted in Mexico City, have been the coin of the realm in California and they were and are still accepted at face value.

So, part of my job, as the Lord's eyes, is to carefully judge the value of each variety of paper and metal offered as money. It's a responsibility that means I have to keep in contact with those who deal all across the county and even the world, so I've made friends with Peter Stanford, who runs Adams Express, and almost daily gets news—although ofttimes old news—from the South and East. I daily devour every newspaper I can get my hands on. The *Mountain Democrat* from Placerville comes to us weekly, but usually a week late; the *Sacramento Daily Union*, usually only a day late; the *New York Tribune*, received normally two months late; the *New Orleans Daily Crescent*, also at least a month late; and the Sydney, Australia, *Sydney Morning Herald*, often three months late. Keeping up on the news is part of my job, and educational, even if ofttimes well behind the times.

I'm careful not to accept too much of any one bank's paper if distant. A bank could fail and we'll not know for two months. So coin is much better.

Keeping up is also expensive as the papers from far away are often a dollar apiece. I read them carefully, refolding, we offer them for resale at the original dollar, or to read for a quarter dollar advising the renter he'll be charged a dollar if not returned in good stead. Most times we get our money back, as those far from home are desperate for news.

I'm pleased that before opening for the day, Beth and Abe return with a receipt from Adams for the full five hundred dollars, not that I expected anything less.

Alice has checked out all possible educational opportunities in the city for Beth and has settled on a private tutor, the wife of a French baker, who is fluent in several languages and has her afternoons to teach languages and other ladylike pursuits. And is only three blocks from The Piccadilly. We have either Abe or Colt walk Beth there for a one o'clock session and one of them hurries over to walk her back at half past three, returning with loaves of wonderful bread, many times still warm from the oven. So it's the proverbial killing two birds with one stone, as bread is served with bowls of beans at low cost to players and drinkers. Even in the well-traveled parts of the city it's not safe for a beautiful young woman to walk the streets alone. I worry it leaves The Piccadilly somewhat exposed without Colt's gun or Abe's muscle, but I think Lord Stanley-Smyth would approve nonetheless.

As well as things are going, I have this ominous

feeling the other shoe is about to drop. The Wallabys are strangely absent. Zeb's killer has still not been found.

As if to justify my concern, Peaches turns up missing. It's been three weeks since a soiled dove was discovered eviscerated, so I'm on the edge of my chair worried about our dove who calls herself Ruth of Sharon, but others call Peaches.

Hopefully she's found a rich suitor and run off, but Alice discovers a stash of nearly one hundred dollars hidden in her room…so that solution is probably false.

I pray for her.

Prayers are not always answered.

In midafternoon, Alex, on duty and in uniform, enters and goes straight to the stairway leading up to my table.

I greet him before he can speak. "You don't look happy."

"No. We found your whore."

14

I'M SILENT A MOMENT, FEARING HIS COMING REPORT, SO Alex continues. "It's the worst as I'm sure you fear. She was discovered in the next alley over, covered with a pile of trash. Gutted like a farmyard pullet. And yes, her knickers were still on. No reason to think the killer a rapist as well. I do believe he just doesn't like filthy whores."

I sigh deeply. "My ladies are clean, Alex. I'll inform Alice and insist none of the ladies leave without another to accompany them."

"She was beaten, beaten badly, so I need you to come identify the body."

It's not a task I look forward to, but I guess my duty, so I nod.

"Please come on, we'd like to get her to the digger," and he leads the way, and over his shoulder adds, "Let's hope two together discourages this whore-hater, and more so hope we catch him first. I'd dearly like to pull the lever on the hangman's scaffold, on this boyo, my very own self." He's saying it, but it doesn't sound sincere.

"Hold on, I'll only be a moment with Alice. You want to come along?"

"I'll not venture into your whorehouse. Never have, never will."

"Be right back," I say, respecting his reticence.

And for the first time since we opened, I head next door to the brothel. I find her in the salon, where she keeps a small desk, and leave her in tears.

I'm happy to say Peaches, laying among garbage, face beaten but also peppered with rat bites, is covered by a scrap of Mr. Goodyear's rubber tent cloth up to her neck. The sight and stench of rotting garbage causes my throat to close. But ignoring my own discomfort, I confirm her identity, assure the coppers we'll pay for her internment and ask them to send the digger to The Piccadilly for his money. Then I get away as quickly as I can, happy they kept me from seeing the horrid gruesome work of the madman, now covered by tent cloth.

The fact the crazy man with the picket who calls himself Elohim is standing at the end of the alley gives me pause, then even more so as he hurries away before I reach him. He's for sure crazy as a rabid raccoon, but crazy enough to kill and gut a woman?

As soon as out of the alley I slow my stride, deep in thought. I'm sure this happened at night, I remember reading somewhere, possibly the Bible, that men who do evil hate the light. My God, and I say that sincerely, how far is what I just saw from the basic tenant of the Bible, of Christianity, from most religions—not all, but most— and that's the Golden Rule, "Do unto others as ye'd have others do unto you."

No matter your belief in the Good Book, in Jesus as

the son of God, in God as to creation, that rule's a belief that all the world, all humanity, should embrace.

But don't.

I'm met at the door by Tom. "Rumors are flying. Is it true?"

"Tis," I reply. And head for the stairs.

Young Beth meets me at the head with the same question. "Is it true?"

"Yes, and you don't want the details. And you're not to leave this place without escort. No matter the circumstance. And I don't mean another lady. Colt, Abe, or even Tom or I will accompany you, or you don't go."

I can see she's taken umbrage at my strong instruction, voiced as a demand not a request, and she backs up a bit.

She straightens almost as if I'd slapped her, and her reply is tart. "I appreciate your concern, Mr. Zane, but I am my own woman, and my aunt Alice is the only one I take personal instruction from. You're the boss of this place and the boss of me so long as I work for you, even if only part time. You're not my father, nor brother, nor teacher or pastor."

I eye her for a moment before I speak, and I speak slowly and deliberately. "Missy, so long as you're under this roof you'll abide by some simple rules. And the first of those when it comes to you is you'll not be on the streets alone."

"Humph," she says, spins on her heel and stomps away.

I watch her leave and wonder; how can a head so pretty be so hard. It's a side of her I haven't seen. And I remember another of my ma's admonitions, pride goes before a fall. I'll have a talk with Miss Alice and make sure Beth and all of Miss Alice's doves are doubly warned.

As if the murder of one of our girls is not enough, shortly after noon, a dozen Wallabys enter. Two at a time as if they won't be noticed.

The last two to enter are easily recognized. Otto Prager, with his ear half bitten away, his girth that of one of Barnabas's mules; and his slim mate, who I remember is Pauly Poundstone, now I know to be nicknamed Tiger —not nicknamed for the mammal but rather for the deadly Australian snake.

Another lone man enters, probably a pistoleer as he, too, wears two revolvers, only his both the size of Navy or Army Colts and each properly seated, butt to the rear. He stays along so I have no idea if he's truly a customer, or a *compadre* of the Wallabys?

I yell down to Flaco Comacho, one of two bartenders on the afternoon shift.

"Flaco, bring me up a mug of suds."

"Busy here," he yells back without looking up, and his barstools are full. And a dozen new customers, only customers I hope, have entered.

So I instruct, "Send Kansas up." Kansas is one of two barmaids and has proven great at her job. She delivers a couple of mugs of suds and ascends the stairs two at a time with the third she's had pulled.

She places it on my table, and comments, "When did you start bellying up?" and spins to go.

It's a fair question as I never have a drink during open hours, and only occasionally after closing.

"Hold on," I yell after her and she stops and turns back.

I lower my voice so those down below cannot hear. "Go out and find a copper. Stay on the main street. I

81

don't want you joining Peaches. Tell him we expect big trouble very soon...the place is full of miscreants...he's to get here with at least a half dozen of his fellow officers."

"Will do," she says, and starts away, but I stop her with another instruction.

"Kansas, do not, and I repeat, do not leave the road outside, not even a side road...stay on the main with lots of good folks in sight."

"Yes, sir," she says, and disappears.

Even though it's a hard sun all morning, our famous fog is beginning to roll in, and maybe a dingy fog is dark enough for this madman lurking in our alleys. But my immediate concern is a room full of the worst of San Francisco's scumbags, and that's saying something in a city now over fifty thousand strong.

My revolver hangs on the back of my chair, and I rise and strap it on. Colt is at his normal chair at the rear end of the bar, a double-barrel Coach gun across his knees, sitting shotgun. He wears a Navy .44 Colt on his right side, and a Sheriff's Model .36-caliber on his left, butt forward. Tennessee Tom has a tall stool, his back against the wall, at a spot halfway between the tables. And of course is also heeled with both a Navy Colt on his hip and a belly gun at his back under his town coat.

As I scan the dozen Wallabys, I'm wishing it was Alex's day off and I had him employed. We may need him and half the police force.

15

Both our working bartenders, Flaco and Dodge, are within steps of Coach guns hidden under the bar. I'm comfortable we could defend the place against a platoon of dragoons should need be, but a gun battle would do little for business should it erupt. And I'm guessing it will.

It seems all the Wallabys are heeled, although a few must have hideout guns as all I can see on a few hips are the foot-long blades and ivory-handled knifes that are their trademark.

I knew this day would come as the Wallabys must defend their reputation as sordid as it is.

Both Colt and Tom are glancing up my way, wondering what the play will be. So I step up to the rail, and shout to the crowd.

"Gentlemen, give me your attention." Things still and all look up my way. I have to repeat it to get the full room's attention. I'd guess there are thirty-five or so at the tables and bar.

"I see we have some new customers, Down Under fellas

who have never visited before." I'm silent a few seconds and get no replies, so I continue. "I'm casting dispersions on no one but want you to know we will close up shop in ten minutes. There's a free beer at the bar for each of you, offered in good faith, knowing you all will leave peacefully."

Then, from the batwings, a roar of a voice erupts. "Bugger you, boyo. This place is comin' apart piece by piece and we're gonna build us a pyre out of these table and chairs, and you are gonna be in the middle of it...just like ol' Joan of Arc."

I'm surprised to see someone I haven't laid eyes on for two years. Ian Burnie, the gang leader, a big man but smaller, at least in weight, since I put an ounce of lead through his knee. Now he has a peg leg, and still a very bad—probably worse—attitude. He's the lout who put a five-hundred-dollar bounty on my head. Rumor had it he'd returned to Australia, but I see now, it was merely a hopeful thought.

I decide to give it right back to him, in spades. "Well, if it isn't old stubby Ian. Word was you'd gone back to live with your mama in the whorehouse she runs in Sydney."

"You're the son of a whore, Jake Zane, and you know I'm blessed by the devil to finally lay eyes on you. I'm gonna—"

I yell to my fellas below, interrupting Burnie. "Gentlemen of The Piccadelly. Have a good look at stubby Ian Burnie. Should any of his flea-bit fellas pull a weapon, ignore them and empty both your barrels into Burnie's fat gut. He's tired of gimpin' about and is dying to meet Beelzebub."

That silences him and everyone else in the room, particularly as Colt steps forward, a revolver in each hand, as Tom climbs off his stool, also swinging the muzzles of two firearms, and as both bartenders shoulder Coach guns. All aimed at Ian.

I lay my Coach gun on the railing, as Ian is cutting his eyes from gunman to gunman.

He yells to his men. "Keep them holstered, fellas. I do believe there'll be another day."

I yell at him again. "Burnie, I know where you can get a job poking holes to plant corn. That peg is good for something." As I'm yelling at him, he's backing out of the batwings. I've been cutting my eyes from him to the fellow I'd pegged—no pun intended—as a shootist. The fancy dressed fella with two smokers on his hip, both butt to the rear. He's been scanning the room, both hands resting on what appears to be bone or ivory grips of shiny nickel revolvers. As I figured, he heads for the batwings and follows Burnie out.

Fact is I'd bet a dollar to a donut he's a hired gun. And a foolish one as we've made him now and will all be on the prod for fancy dan.

"The rest of you pig lickin' Wallabys follow your mates."

"How about them free beers?" one of them shouts.

"I didn't know you'd brought butt-lick Burnie or I'd never offered," I shout back, and am pleased to note they're all moving toward the door. As soon as they clear out, Tom and Colt find the stairway and are soon at my table.

Tom is shaking his head. "Boy, you do know how to rub salt in the wound."

"He's cost me many nights of sleep and it's not over. Should I find him without a gang of lapdogs at his side, I'd call him out. He's got a five-hundred-dollar bounty on my head, and every back shootin' yellow dog in San Francisco would like to collect."

Tom eyes me with a cold smile. "Hell, five hundred. That's more tempting than that two floors of sweet doves next door."

"Very amusing, Tennessee."

He laughs and heads back to the stairway. I start to laugh, but then realize I'm not too damn sure he's not serious.

Colt raps a knuckle on the table and gets my attention. "You go out, I go along."

"I'm not one of the ladies," I snap.

"Lady, man, or buffalo, an ounce of lead will bring you down. You go, I go."

I laugh. "Fair enough, friend."

Understanding Lord Stanley-Smyth's instruction, I've not become too friendly with any of The Piccadilly employees, even Miss Alice or Tennessee Tom. It's been more difficult where Beth is concerned. It seems she must have had a heart-to-heart with her aunt as she has accepted my edict that she never, never, never go out to the street alone, only with a man, an armed man, as escort.

She's again at my table, as we check each other's count of the take from the day before, our conflab between Alice, Tom, and myself has concluded, but Tom returns.

"Judged by the crowds I'd say our take has fallen by half," he says, and I can see he has something on his mind.

"You're a good judge," I reply.

"Both of our main competition, Parker's Palace and Frisco Fred's, have entertainment and the ladies are a dollar a flop—"

"You get what you pay for," I interrupt, and notice Beth blushing.

"True, but the fact is our take is down. I'd like to hire some entertainment?"

"Worth a try," I say.

And Beth, with nary a bit of humility, offers, "I sing."

"Most all ladies do, Miss Beth," Tom says, with a smile and prompt dismissal. Then adds, "We need more than someone from a church choir."

She persists. "Did you know Temple, your dealer, is a fine piano player?"

Tom sighs, then replies. "Temple would make much more as a dealer than a piano player."

"I mean only for an audition. The least you can do is give me a chance?"

I smile, as doubtful as Tom seems to be, but nod at him. "The least."

"No matter," he says, "we'll need a piano. The *Allegany* that docked yesterday, has posted her freight for sale, and I noticed a piano among the haul. How about I go to the dock and haggle with Parker-Stiles, their agent?"

"Time we stepped up our game," I say. "Buy it cheap."

"Yes," Beth says, "but buy one that is a fine instrument. Even if not me, no entertainer will work backed by an instrument out of tune or incapable of being tuned."

I laugh as she sounds as if she knows of which she speaks. So I suggest, "Miss Beth, I suggest you accompany Tom and give your approval before he squanders our hard-earned."

"My pleasure," she says.

Tom shakes his head, seemingly a little disgusted, then relents. "Let's not tarry as it'll sell. Give me time to admonish the dealers to keep an eye on each other, in case we don't return before opening."

"I'll get my parasol," Beth says, and hurries to the door to the brothel side.

"Barnabas is back from the Sierra. Don't let them charge you for delivery should you be successful. We'll send for him and a freight wagon."

He waves over his shoulder and descends the stairs.

Seems we're to not only be saloon, gambling establishment, and brothel, but now an opera house. Come to think of it, we came very close to being Rome's Colosseum, as with a dozen Wallabys the saloon floor came very close to being a battleground.

And Alex informed me, as I treated him and a couple of his fellow officers to a whiskey last night, that the Wallabys were released that very day from jail on the trumped-up charge of disturbing the peace.

What next?

16

WITH THE PIANO DELIVERED AND OUR TALENTED DEALER reporting before opening, Tom, Alice, and myself are stationed near the back of the saloon, coffee cups in hand. Temple is trying out our nearly new upright Chickering and Sons piano. Alice has assured us Beth will soon appear and we're enjoying, and surprised at, Temple's playing while waiting.

Alice informs us, and surprises me at least, relating that Beth attended a music school in Chicago, and is not only skilled—or so says her aunt—in voice but also in violin.

As the dealers and bartenders are preparing for the days business there's a slight hum in the room with polishing tables, stacking chips, and polishing and placing glasses and mugs.

The room goes dead silent, making both Tom and I wonder if there's not trouble at our batwings and we both turn in our chairs. My jaw drops as Beth, looking as if she's just stepped off a stage in New York, approaches. She's dressed in a full-length gown, scooped at the neck just low enough to be proper. She's carrying a polished violin in one hand and sheet music in the other and strolls directly to the piano and hands the music to Temple, who takes and studies it for a moment.

She leans near Temple, "Can you do those?"

He gives her a confident smile, but then says, "I may miss a note or two, but the way you look no one will notice."

She gives him a smile and nod, then requests, "Let's start with 'Swanee'." Then back to us. "This is likely the kind of music your crowd will enjoy."

Before she's through the first verse, both Tom and I have collapsed back in our chairs, jaws dropped. She's an angel. Her aunt Alice has the coyest of smiles on her beautiful face. Beth finishes, then instructs, "Please go on to 'Ave Maria'." Again turning to us, she explains, "'Ave Maria' is a piece by Schubert from 1825. It's actually a prayer, written to the words of Sir Walter Scott's epic poem *Lady of the Lake*. I hope you enjoy."

We're even more astounded, but the instant she finishes she tucks the violin under her chin and plays the melody.

Awestruck, we forget to applaud as she lets the violin hang at one side and the bow at the other.

"Did I do something wrong?" she asks, looking perplexed.

Only then do I realize the other three dealers, bartender, two barmaids, and Abe have slipped up behind us and are as enraptured as are we.

We all break out in laughter, then applause nearly rattles the windows.

Now Beth blushes.

Still smiling I turn to her audience. "Get at it, ladies

and gentlemen. We open in fifteen minutes." And they return to work.

Then I center attention on Beth again. "And what would two appearances per evening, say fifteen to twenty minutes each cost the establishment?"

She shrugs, but Aunt Alice does not. "Five dollars per," she says quickly.

It's my duty, watching over the Lord's money, so I negotiate. "Three dollars each."

Beth loses her shyness. "Four dollars per and I'll double your crowd."

"Three dollars plus a dime for every warm body over our normal forty who walks through our door."

Alice is no fool, and steps in again. "Charge a cover of two bits on the nights she sings, say Wednesday, Friday, and Saturday—no cover after her last show. Beth takes the cover after the first three dollars. No risk to you."

"Only if we get no crowd because of the twenty-five cent cover charge," I reply.

"Try it two weeks, then we'll renegotiate."

I nod, and shake hands with both Alice and Beth, not a normal male-female event, but negotiating with females is abnormal. Tom does likewise, shaking.

But he adds, "I'll lose money if the gambling stops while she performs."

So I reply, "And you'll make a lot more should the crowd double." I change the subject as Tom seems miffed. "I was wondering why we don't have a wheel-of-chance?"

"Could," Tom says, "but it would have to be under the balcony, out of your watchful eye, unless we move a faro table there."

"But not your hawk gaze. Besides, I imagine hard to cheat with a wheel-of-chance."

"Younger," he says, "if there's a game, gamblers will figure how to cheat."

"See if you can find an honest wheel and I'll find the money."

He nods, and I'm nearly alone as Alice and Beth have left as well.

Temple stands with hands on hips. "You got a piano player maybe to deal with as well."

"You're paid by the hour, bartending or playing piano."

He gives me a disgusted, "Humph," then adds. "Bartending don't take much talent and while I'm beatin' the keys I ain't getting tips."

"Good point," I admit. "How about a dollar a session, in addition to your wages."

He spits in his palm and reaches out to shake. So I follow suit and the deal is made.

Now, if our young songbird can draw a crowd. I have a very good feeling she'll pack the place.

We decide the first show will be at seven p.m. when the place is normally as busy as it will be, as the early birds—most of whom come in as businesses close up and down the road—leave by seven or eight, and the latecomers arrive from seven to ten.

A roar erupts at seven when we close the tables, even announcing we have a little entertainment for the next twenty minutes. The good news is players swamp the barmaids and the two bartenders at work.

I announce Beth from the railing of the balcony where we've decided she'll perform, even though the piano is directly below on the saloon floor. I have trouble getting the crowd to quiet down, but they immediately go silent as the first pure notes flow out of the songbird. Her voice is not only pure, but powerful. She starts again with "Swanee" and by the time she's halfway through "Ave Maria," I survey the crowd, realizing all but a few have removed their hats, and a few have tears rolling down their cheeks. Tears! I've cried, but not in public. Not among a bevy of the toughest men on earth. Beth is not only a hit but seems to be loved by the crowd. What else but love could silence a room full of rough drovers, sailors, teamsters, townsmen, and construction workers…nothing but love and respect?

She does two instrumentals alone on her violin and five songs accompanied by Temple on the piano. When it's time for her to return for a nine o'clock set, I have no problem quieting the crowd. Those who stood through the first show handle that job for me, I even hear three or four fellas threaten to throw another out into the road if he doesn't button his lip when she's about to begin.

Temple, at first when I heard him practicing—on his own time—I wondered if we'd need to find a more accomplished musician. But he has risen to the occasion. After the second set he bounds up the stairs and, in his enthusiasm, gives Beth a big hug, and she blushes with the continued applause and his exuberance. Then he comes to me and insists, "We must hire another violinist to play while she sings and maybe a flutist. I can arrange—"

I stop him with my laughter, and he looks a little hurt until I agree. "I'll be surprised if we don't have to turn them away at the door before her performance tomorrow evening. But please, on your off time, find some talent to audition."

The fact is I have rumor of the mercantile next door closing—the side opposite the brothel—as the proprietor is having trouble finding help. All able-bodied men are still clamoring toward the goldfields, and he wants to go himself. If I can buy the building cheaply enough, we can sell or auction off the merchandise and it's big enough to seat over a hundred. I envision the Piccadilly Theater. There's only a three-foot-wide passageway between the buildings so it could be easily connected to the saloon.

We'll see how she does on her next show. My growing admiration for her, and to be truthful, attraction to her, may be clouding my judgment. Lord Stanley-Smyth would advise, when first glance at something mesmerizes you, it's time to walk away and come back another day for another look.

And Beth, even if a bit hardheaded, has totally entranced me.

17

BETH HAS SUNG FOR TWO WEEKS, AND THIS MORNING I paid her eighteen dollars for her two performances. She's making twice what our dealers and bartenders are pulling down, more than most the soiled doves.

I'm surprised we haven't had trouble with the Wallabys, and when Alex stops by for his nightly on-the-house whiskey, I question him. "We have not seen those worthless louts, the Wallabys?"

"I should have kept you informed. You're not shed of the vermin. However, they've been busy with their own troubles. The Sharks, another growing gang of no-accounts made up of Australians from the Perth side, a few Sandwich Islanders, a few Samoans, are trying to push them out of their territory. Eight dead so far from their territorial feuds."

"The coppers can't stop them?" I ask.

He chuckles. "And put the judges and hangman to work. Marshal Willowby says so long as the killing is all Wallabys and Sharks, let 'em have at it."

That gives me a chuckle, so I add, "So long as they

stay away from The Piccadilly, let them have at it. Hell's bells, I'll send over some shot and powder should it help them along."

"I need a favor?" Alex asks.

"If it's in my power," I reply.

"Willowby and his missus, and a couple of our judges and their ladies, would like to attend one of Beth's songfests?"

"In here...in The Piccadilly?"

"Unless you have a better idea?"

I put my chin in hand and think for a moment as he takes a long draw of his whiskey, then do have an idea. "The Metropolitan is going dark next week as tomorrow is the last night for the play *De Soto*. Why don't we make a night of it. The Piccadilly will rent the place, if possible, hire their orchestra. They charge an astronomical one buck to five for seats. I bet I can make money at half that, and give away two dozen seats to the city's finest, and I'll let you hand those tickets to Willowby to give to whomever he pleases."

"And the ladies won't have to risk their reputations entering a saloon—"

"And I won't have to run the riffraff out so they can do so."

Alex laughs. "You do know how to make friends."

Hearing a shout, I turn to see Tennessee Tom crack a skinny fellow over the head with his pistol. The fellow's pard is reaching for his sidearm as he feels the cold muzzle of Colt Barberosa's sidearm shoved just under his ear.

Alex, in uniform, starts that way but I grab his upper arm. "Let them handle it. They've had little to do since Beth started singing. Dang if no one wants to be thrown out and miss the show. The last two nights we had to post Abe and Colt at the door to turn fellas away."

As we talk, our backs to the bar, Colt and Tom, having disarmed both the troublemakers—we hold confiscated weapons until the next day—march them by and give them a hefty shove out through the batwings.

They are heading back to their positions, only twenty feet from the door, when the one Tom had smacked with his revolver bursts back in with a pocket gun in hand, swinging it back and forth looking for his target.

To my great surprise, as I'm yelling at Tom and Abe to look out, Alex has a six-shot Allen's pepperbox in hand and fires. The intruder spins and goes to his face on the floor.

He's unmoving. The .36-caliber ball hit him in the temple and I'd guess him dead before he hit the floor.

Both Tom and Colt walk over and extend their hand to Alex.

Colt mumbles as he shakes. "Never thought I'd be in debt to a copper."

"You're not," Alex says. "My duty."

But Tom disagrees. "The hell you say, Officer Alex. That's the second time you've come to our aid. We're indebted. Call on us anytime."

"How about now…haul that bloke out to the board-walk. I'll bet my lads are running this way. Send them in and we'll get him on his way to the digger."

Alex just laughs as both Tom and Colt give him a nod, and turns back to me.

I've been waiting to ask him and do as Tom and Colt drag the body out. "Anything new on the madman?"

"Nothing. He leaves no evidence, and it seems no one puts pressure on the department as one witness I talked to said, they're only whores."

I shake my head in disgust. "They've got mas and pas and some even children. Somebody cares."

"Truthful, somebody steals an apple from an upstanding merchant and it gets more attention than a whore getting murdered."

"Not right," I say.

"Maybe not, but that's the way it is. They reap what they sew."

I should chastise him for that remark but remain silent. I'm in thought a moment, then ask another question that's been bothering me. "How about Zeb's children. They doing alright?"

"Don't know. His wife had folks in Sacramento, and they lit out for there."

"I hope they're doing alright," I say, and notice Temple closing down his table and heading for the piano. I excuse myself from Alex and the bar, and head for the stairway, wanting to catch Beth before she performs.

And as I top the stairs, she's coming through the door to the brothel from the quarters she shares with her aunt.

"Good evening," she says, with a halfhearted smile.

"And to you. What's wrong?"

"Not a thing."

"I've been invited to an appreciation night at Adams Express and can bring a guest. I don't suppose…"

She lights up with big smile. "I have a new gown. Is this affair stylish enough I can wear it and show off a little?"

"You'd be the prettiest girl there in a flour sack."

"Why, Mr. Zane, that's the nicest thing you said in a month of Sundays."

"I haven't known you a month of Sundays, but it's the God's honest truth. Is Miss Alice in the salon?"

"She is, and I suspect you'll be asking her permission."

"You know me too well. Time for you to go to work," I say with a mock serious demeanor.

She heads for the railing, and I enter the brothel for about the third time since it has opened. I'm a little surprised to see Alice in conversation with Marshal Willowby and Judge Ogden Hoffman, our local federal judge.

Both the judge and marshal look a little embarrassed as I approach, then the judge announces, "Doing a little city business here. Don't get the wrong impression…"

18

"Gentlemen," I say, and they look a little surprised as it's well known I normally stay on my side of the brothel door.

I let them off the hook with, "Sorry to interrupt your business conversation. May I borrow Miss Alice for a moment?"

"Yes," the judge says, then stammers a little, "discussing these killings of doves."

"Yes, sir. I assumed something like that." Then I turn to Alice. "A moment, then I'll let you return."

She rises and follows me back to the door. "What's so important?"

"I'm invited to a customer open house at Adams's tomorrow evening, and have asked Beth to accompany—"

She laughs. "You don't need my permission to court—"

I feel my face redden. "Not courting, Miss Alice. Merely an evening out to enjoy some fine fixins and music with friends."

"Call it what you will," she says, laughing again. "Have a good time. I'll expect her back by the witching hour."

"Won't be that late," I say, still a little red in the face.

"Have a nice time," she says, and goes back to her table.

I slip around behind Beth, who's well into "Farewell My Lilly Dear," and as quietly as possible I descend the stairs. Temple has still not found a flutist nor a violinist, explaining that only working three nights a week does not appeal to those who can work seven at other establishments should they wish to.

But it doesn't seem to matter. Beth fills the house on Wednesdays, Fridays, and Saturdays.

She now closes each performance with "Ave Maria," still drawing a few tears, and I fear the house will come down around our ears with the shouts, applause, and stomping of feet as they try to get her to continue. Someone threw a coin up onto the balcony at her third performance and now at the close of each, coins sail over the railing but she does not disdain to gather them, so it's become a ritual for Abe, who she tips generously.

We are only four days from her performing at the Metropolitan, which I've rented for the princely sum of two hundred fifty dollars for the night, plus another fifty-five for the ten-piece orchestra and conductor to lead them. They are to accompany her with fifteen selections, twelve vocals and three with her on the violin.

I'm to get my costs back—and as or more important, more goodwill with Marshal Willowby, Judge Hoffman, Mayor Silver Chastine, and other city officials—and she'll get the balance should there be any excess. With the number of seats, if she fills the place, she'll make over two hundred dollars for the night. If Beth has any interest in me, I may be cutting my courting throat, making her a wealthy woman who'll have little need of a husband. For the first time I realize that I'm having deep feelings for Elizabeth.

Every Monday I write Lord Stanley-Smyth at the London address he left me, reporting the events of their prior week and the take. Should business continue as it has been, I'll have to look for a second bank as having too much deposited in one seems a fool's errand. I recall him saying Mugsy was the missus's cat, but he seemed awfully attached to her. And to be truthful so am I. I haven't had a body sleeping next to me since traveling on the Oregon Trail and then I normally slept in a hammock under the wagon and only ventured inside it's protective canvas cover if storming terribly. And it's nice having some company as I've tried to respect the Lord's instruction, and that's having workmates and employees respect you, not necessarily befriend you. Since taking care of Mugsy, she has become my best friend. The only time I've been cross with Mugsy is when she placed a rat, still twitching, on my chest. I awakened to a very proud cat purring, a rat twitching, and me yelling as if a full-fledged fire-eating dragon was astraddle me.

I scared her into flight as if her tail was afire and in three steps was on my deck flinging a rat far out into the dark alley.

I've yet to get a return letter from the Lord but am sure it's ten months or twice that to get mail from England—although he said he might remain in New York—it's around the horn by ship, and unless he wrote me before receiving my first letter, it could take more than a year and a few months for a reply.

He did instruct me to send a draft each time our Adams deposits exceed three thousand dollars, and I've already sent two. I have no way to know if he's received but will continue sending. I'd wager our take is ten times that of the prior establishment, the Bucket of Blood.

I've taken the liberty of borrowing his coach, which has been stored with Barnabas and Max, the hostler at Kingdom Freight and Mail Company, which the Lord also owns.

I'm taking liberties I haven't discussed with the Lord, but he's in London, and as mentioned, a little difficult to reach.

For the first time I'm wishing there was another entrance to Alice's Pleasure Parlour, as it is I'll have to either escape the bordello through the alley entrance, or escort Beth down the stairs and through the saloon.

So I await her in the brothel salon to give her the choice.

Escorted by her aunt, who again seems amused, she walks from her quarters in a floor-length robin's-egg blue gown, with matching parasol and feathered hat, and is breathtaking. "Do you approve?" she asks, and slowly does a complete three-hundred-and-sixty-degree turn, before I can get my wits about me.

"There aren't words..." I manage, then do give her the choice of our exit. I'm surprising her with the coach and Barnabas as driver.

She asks, "Do we have a hack or are we walking ten blocks?"

"We can find a ride at the saloon door, or I can have our ride directed to the alley?"

"Sir, I didn't spend a half day dressing to sneak out through the alley."

"Then let's bedazzle the boys at the bar," I say, and we both laugh.

She takes my arm, we cross the balcony, and are only halfway down the stairway when the place goes so silent you could hear a pin drop as all eyes are on her. I quickly discover I enjoy being envied. Men snatch their hats off and part, leaving a path as we approach, and she smiles and nods to men on either side. Colt has seen us coming and leads a few feet in front and holds a batwing open as we exit.

"Oh, my," she says, seeing the coach and Barnabas holding its door for her, and offering a hand to help her up. "I've never..." she begins.

But I shush her. "Your carriage should be trimmed in gold and silver."

She laughs.

I continue, "I know a few of the folks who'll be at this shindig, but not near all. Peter, my friend who's our host, and the manager of this Adams, will introduce us around."

But to be truthful, I wonder what our reception will be. The newspapers have covered Beth's performances well, which I've been happy about, but also noted that she was a resident of Alice's Pleasure Parlour.

I'm watching the city streets carefully through the open coach window, and shouldn't be surprised, but am, when I see Colt on a saddle horse—he must have arranged with Barnabas—riding not far behind us.

He told me I wasn't going to be on the street without him near, and he's taken his own initiative to make sure I'm not.

I like having a cat, I love having a beautiful woman on my arm, and to be truthful—with a cutthroat gang like the Wallabys after me—I kinda like having a skilled shootist watching my back.

19

ADAMS HAS A SPACIOUS OFFICE AND AT ITS REAR IS A BARN large enough to accommodate six Concord coaches and at least twenty mules and horses. The barn's been cleaned out and all but the stalls have been covered with wooden pallets and in turn with Chinese carpets, two dozen colorful Chinese paper lanterns hang from the cross rafters. I'm amazed at the work gone into this party, then again Adams has long been transporting millions of dollars of gold from the fields and a fair chunk of that stays in their coffers. Peter and his wife Madaline occupy one of the city's most beautiful homes on Nob Hill, overlooking city and bay.

There are ten round tables and six rectangular ones, seating well over a hundred. At the alley entrance, two large pits are surrounded with adobe bricks and two halves of beef and two lambs turn over a bed of coals. A second pit has two pigs, each at least a hundred pounds, dripping over hot coals.

Between them and the seating are two long tables with plates of fruits and vegetables, crab, and oysters.

At the far office end is a ten-piece orchestra, playing demurely as folks arrive.

Peter, with his wife in tow, meet us as we exit the office into what's now an elegant party space, even with the lingering odor of a barnyard.

Madaline is as sweet and kind as I've known her to be, the couple of times I've been invited to dine at their home.

But I notice those already at the party and those arriving after us, seem to be avoiding us as if we have the plague. Then, on my way to get Beth and Madaline a glass of punch, I overhear a couple of older women talking, and realize why. I hear, "...yes, pretty enough, but she's a strumpet, living in a brothel. Her aunt's the madam. And he's a gambler and owns...or at least runs, that evil place...I wouldn't let..."

And I move along. Peter invites us to share his table, and I'm pleased that Willowby, Judge Hoffman, and the town mayor, Silver Chastine, are seated there, with their wives. The women each give Beth a nod, but that's the extent of it. They rudely ignore her, so I them.

Now I'm embarrassed. Not that the most beautiful woman at the party has accompanied me, but rather that I've put her through the embarrassment of surrounding her with a bunch of what I consider pompous asses who I consider as wicked as Satan himself.

I make sure to include Beth in the men's conversation and give the women, I won't say ladies, my back as much as possible.

Each table has a ring of six candles at its center, and inside that ring is a bouquet of flowers. As we finish our dessert, some excellent pudding made with expensive vanilla beans from deep in Mexico, a blast of wind rustles through the barn, and the three candles on the side of four of the obnoxious women are blown out.

I immediately take the opportunity to make a toast with the excellent red wine that's been served to each of us. The women all consent to raise their glasses when I propose, then almost choke when I say, "Directly from the Bible, which I imagine you're all familiar with, Proverbs I believe, 'For there shall be no reward to the evil woman; the candle of the wicked shall be put out.'" I take the liberty of changing gender, man to woman. They all toast, looking a little confused, then at least one of the women gets it and chokes on her wine. The men pay no attention, happy to have an excuse for another swig.

"May I get you some water," Beth speaks to her for the first time since being introduced.

The woman, her cloth napkin to her reddening cheeks, shakes her head.

We excuse ourselves before the party concludes. Peter walks us outside and as soon as we enter the offices on our way to the street, stops us. He speaks directly to Beth. "Miss Beth, Madaline and I were so very proud to have you here. We'll be in the front row on Tuesday when you sing." He's silent a moment, and I know he's searching for words, then offers, "You know the saying—ignorance is bliss. Well, young lady, you've just witnessed some of the most blissful women on the west coast."

Beth smiles that brilliant smile as Peter brushes his lips over her extended hand. But at the same time, a tear rolls down her cheek, and I detect her catching a sob.

"Thank you, a grand party," I say, and we're gone.

As we're reseated in the coach, her staring out the window, I'm compelled to ask, "Did I do wrong invit-

ing...I had no idea...I'm sorry you had to go through...
damn hypocrites."

I get a smile equal to that she gave Peter. Then she
again stares out at the dark city as she speaks. "My
sainted mother always said, when life hands you lemons
make lemonade. And that many of us make our Hell
right here on earth. Those women stew in their own
broth."

I return the smile, but then it fades. "Miss Elizabeth,
you are wise beyond your years."

She turns back to me and laughs. "I've noticed that
about you, Jake Zane."

When we exit, I'm not surprised to see Barnabas and
Colt seated near the door, each smoking a stogie. They
snuff them out seeing us, and Barnabas beats us to the
coach and has the door open and a hand out to help
Beth.

I have Miss Beth returned—overpaying Barnabas a
shiny five-dollar gold piece, and telling Barnabas I'll buy
him a box of the cigars he relishes—to her aunt before
ten, much less well before the witching hour.

That's the good news, the bad is Miss Alice greets me
with, "Jade, one of my Orientals, is missing."

"But she's not a dove," I can't help but voice.

"She was dressed modestly, as always, but walked out
the back door of the Pleasure Parlour."

"Alone?" I can't help but ask with an accusatory tone.

"She wasn't a dove...you said..." But she looks very
worried.

"All ladies, from now on," I say, then add, "I hope
that's not closing the barn door after the stock has
escaped."

"I pray so," Beth says, and heads for her quarters.

I CAN'T HELP but suspect the crazy man who calls himself Elohim. He's older, wears sandals, supposedly religious and a religious man—at least you'd think—and is not one who'd murder and do such heinous acts as eviscerating one he killed. That said, many wars have been fought, many thousands, maybe millions, have been killed in the name of religion. I can't help but get him out of my thoughts.

Saturday is uneventful, with a packed house, nary a fist fight or even loud argument. That's the good news, the bad is Jade has not returned. Sunday, I'm waiting for the other shoe to drop, and just before midnight I'm wondering if it has as two Wallabys wander in, and a few feet behind them is the same well-dressed fella, who we'd made as a shootist—wearing two guns on his hip— that had been here the night a dozen showed up with the boss of the gang, peg leg Ian Burnie. The shootist wears a hat with a brim as flat as a billiard table and a brocade vest full of silver threads. He's hard to miss, but apparently is confident enough he's not hiding. He heads for the bar and stands eying the mirrors, so he knows what goes on behind. The Wallabys find seats at a faro table.

As soon as they clear the door, Sergeant Alex O'Toole and two of his officers push their way through the batwings. The two coppers remain on the saloon floor, but Alex goes straight to the stairway and joins me.

"I saw them enter," he says. "Figured they came to make trouble...we know who the fancy fellow is?"

20

"I'D LIKE TO KNOW?"

"Sam McFadden, known to many as Sudden Sam, I presume as he's quick to pull a weapon. Rumor is he's in the employ of Ian Burnie and the Wallabys."

"I'm sure you've looked to see if there's a flyer on him?"

"We got nothing. Don't mean there is nothing, but we got nothing."

"So," I say, quietly, studying the man at the bar, "he's nothing more than another customer…a well-heeled one, but so far just a customer. Let's go down and say howdy, welcome to The Piccadilly."

"Suits me," Alex says, and we head for the stairs.

Tom's big hound, Tor, has been dozing near my table, but takes up our tail. As soon as he hits the bottom stair, he stops, eyeing the room, and growling.

The man called Sudden Sam is only three stools from Colt, and I can see they're in conversation. The men at the bar between them seem to melt away from their stools, leaving them empty. I see one stop a fella heading to take up one of the stools. He whispers to the man and the fella spins on his heel and they both walk away. Leaving the three stools vacant.

Sudden Sam has a hand on a revolver, Colt is tapping the muzzle of his Coach gun on the bar, not pointing it at Sam but not far from doing so. As we approach, I can see he has both barrels cocked.

Tor, the hound, is taking it all in, the hair up on his back, his displeasure a low rumble in his throat.

"You two having trouble?" I ask as we near.

Colt answers without taking his eyes off of Sam. "Old chums, Jake. We worked together on the *Memphis Belle*. Sam here had to kill a few fellas making trouble, till he was discharged for being a little too friendly with his sidearms. Shot a couple of them fellas in the back, didn't ya, Sam?"

Sam growls, "That's a rumor, Barberosa. And you know damn well it is. You weren't there—"

"I wasn't there," I interrupt, then continue, "I'm guessing your palm is itching as your rubbing it on that bone grip on your six-shooter. You should know several of us are nervous, having such a famous fella in the house. Suggest you take your hand off the bone and wrap it around a whiskey." I yell at Dodge, who's noticed what's happening and has moved down the bar, one hand resting on one of the Coach guns hidden thereunder. "Hey, Dodge, bring Mr. Sam here three fingers of our best, on the house."

He eyes me, his eyes narrow, his lips as tight as a snake, then challenges, "And if I don't?"

I smile broadly and step forward and slap him on a shoulder in a friendly way. "I hear you're fast, Sudden Sam, but I wonder if you're as fast as Tennessee Tom over yonder who already has a pistol drawn, or can put a pill in Mr. Barberosa here before Alex and his three fellow officers can draw and fire, or before my bartenders down the way there can grab those Coach guns under the bar, each a double-barrel and each barrel loaded with a dozen or so .25-caliber balls...or for that matter before my friend Sergeant Alex here, or I, can put three or four in your brisket, not that we're as fast as you are reputed to be...but you will be busy."

Alex backs me up with, "Sam, you'll look just fine strapped to a plank, pennies on your eyes, a couple of dozen holes in your brisket, leaning up against the undertaker's shop for a few days, as an example of what San Francisco thinks of shootists."

Sam manages a, "Humph," but then looks the bar and saloon over. He gives me a tight-lipped nod, turns and lays both hands flat on the bar, then yells at Dodge, "Hey, you fat bugger face, where's my whiskey?"

I say to his back. "Just one, Mr. McFadden, then I'd appreciate you making room at the bar, in fact in the saloon, for other customers. And take those two low-life Wallabys with you."

He nods, and says without turning, "Obliged for the whiskey. Should I see you on the street I'll pay you back. We'll see how friendly you are without a half-dozen backups." He downs the whiskey Dodge has placed before him in one gulp, then heads for the faro table to gather up his chums.

I can see the Wallabys grousing at him as they leave. They must have been winning.

I feel like patting myself on the back. I've avoided another gun battle in The Piccadilly as, one of the great understatements, they are very bad for business.

The rest of the night is uneventful...but the morning is not.

Miss Alice shows up at our morning meeting with Lily, Jade's mother, in tow. Lily's English is not so good, so Alice speaks for her. Tom, seated at the table, seems very interested in what's transpiring. Tor lays at his side, the sleepy look on his gray mug does not fool me. I've been around the hound enough to know he misses nothing.

"Thank God, Jade is not a victim of that madman... however, she was kidnapped and they want a ransom."

I'm silent for a moment, taking this news in. Then asked, "They who?"

"We can find that out right now. A young Chinese fellow, a messenger, is due to be waiting at our door."

I move the railing and shout down to Dodge, who's checking stock at the bar. "Dodge, a Chinaman is at the door. Fetch him up, please."

He does, but doesn't bother to escort him, merely points him to the stairway. Before he tops it, Lily awaits him, screaming what I suppose are expletives. The Chinaman has stopped halfway up the stairway. I turn to Alice, "Call her off if we want to learn anything."

Alice strides over and takes Lily by the arm and leads her back to the table. She seats her, shushes her, and goes to meet the young Chinese fellow, then escorts him to the table where he remains standing. He's wearing a dirt or food spotted overshirt that extends almost to his knees, floppy pants, also of white cotton, a black sash into which is seated a small hatchet, is pock-faced— probably from surviving small pox—and has a braided queue hanging down to midback. He's obviously been slopping through a badly tended street as his sandaled feet and pants a foot above the sandals are stained with mud and manure. As he approaches Tor stands, and his growl is ominous. I about decide the young Chinaman is

113

going to turn and run, but Tom chastises Tor and the hound flops down next to his chair.

The big dog and Mugsy, my cat, have never made peace, and Mugsy leaps from my lap and slinks off. I guess Tor too close for her liking.

The Chinaman stands with hands folded behind his back and speaks as if he's memorized his delivery. But his eyes only glance quickly away from Tor, who's eyeing his every move. He hardly looks our way from watching Tor's every twitch.

He stutters a little trying to deliver his message. "G... G...Gum San Tong has rescued China girl. Want one thousand dollar, gold, for glorious task."

Lily starts screaming at him again until Alice covers her mouth with a hand. When she's silenced, I respond.

"You're name?" I ask.

"Fat Fang," he says.

Were it not so serious, I'd burst out laughing. But Tom saves me by speaking up.

"Fat is a common Chinese surname. One of the cooks I knew in New Orleans was named Fat Yi...you know given names are last so Fat is a family name."

"Thank you," I say, and mean it as even as long as I've been in San Francisco with its large Chinese population, I've learned little of the culture. I do know they can be mean and tough and had occasion to come against them in the past.

I turn back to the young man. "Okay, Fat Fang, how did it happen you rescued Miss Jade."

He looks confused, then Lily rattles off a string of Chinese words, I guess translating. He replies and she turns to me. "He say no matter how. They have Jade and demand one thousand dollars for her release."

21

I CHEW ON THAT A MOMENT, THEN TO LILY SAY, "TELL HIM that is a great deal of money and it will take us a while to obtain it."

While she's translating, I walk to the rail and shout down to Dodge, "Where's our swamper." I don't want to use Abe's name.

"Cellar, I believe. Want me to fetch him?"

"Please, tell him to wait behind the door."

"What?" Dodge says, looking up at me like I'm a suit short in a deck.

"Like I said," I say, in a more demanding tone. Dodge shrugs and heads for the cellar stairs. Then I turn to Lily. "Does he understand?"

"He do," she replies. "He say he return before sun goes down."

"No, in the morning," I instruct. "Tell him we need tonight's receipts."

Alice has been shifting in her seat nervously, and snaps at me, "Between us girls we have enough next door—"

115

I give her a look that would melt candle wax, and she shuts up. She's speaking the same time Lily is translating, so I'm sure Fat Fang has not understood her and he's paying careful attention to Lily.

He nods, spins on his sandal heel, and heads for the stairway. I follow him closely and give him a chance to get halfway to the batwings before opening the door to the cellar stairs. As instructed, Abe is waiting there.

"Abe, no questions. A young Chinese just left, white shirt and pants, black sash, turned right. Follow him. Don't be seen. Report back where he goes."

Abe nods and hurries to the door, hesitates just looking outside, then waves over his shoulder and disappears outside.

"It barracoon," Lily said, looking at me as if I'd just slit Jade's throat, "and sell Jade we no pay."

The thought of the barracoon makes me clinch my jaw. "I know the barracoon, I dealt with them two years ago." I think for a minute as they all await my solution to the problem. Then I say very deliberately, "Fellas like this Gum San Tong get a taste, they'll want the whole bottle. It'll just happen again we don't put an end to it." I go to the rail and again yell at Dodge. "Please find a copper and ask him to fetch Alex here."

"Yes, sir," he yells back and disappears outside.

Alice looks a little perplexed, and asks, "What the devil is a barracoon?"

"No slavery in California, right?" I ask.

"I presume not," she replies.

"So there damn sure is. Have you taken a stroll down Dupont...Chinatown?"

She puffs up a little, "Of course not, I was advised to leave Chinatown to the Chinese."

So I explain, "There are at least two barracoons in Chinatown. Ships land with Chinese girls and they're sold, auctioned off just like the slave markets in the south."

She puffs up again. "That's not legal."

I nod, "True, but cross enough palms with enough silver and much of what's not legal is ignored."

She's puzzling this all out. "So, this Gum San Tong owns a barracoon and has Jade?"

"They do, and have their headquarters there...and likely have Jade there. I'm sure they think they can get more from us than from an auction or they wouldn't have tried us."

I turn to Tom. "You see any reason they can't get a devil of a bunch more from us?"

"How about four Coach gun loads and a dozen or so sidearms."

Alice's jaw drops. "You'll be in the middle of two thousand Chinese. I'm sure there will be a small army of hard, well-armed Chinamen there."

I nod and risk a little cockiness. "And a half dozen of us, well-armed, are worth four dozen Celestials. I won't have you buying back your ladies every time some tong needs a few dollars. Besides, we'll have the coppers on our side."

"Don't count on it," she offers.

"How so?" I ask, a little incredulously.

"Word is the coppers won't go down Dupont. Rumor is they are paid well to stay away."

"Then they won't see us slinging lead at a bevy of gentlemen with long braids."

Alice can't help but give me a tight smile, then says, "Jake Zane, you do have a way of looking on the bright side of things, even when it comes to spilling a lot of blood. I want to go on record, the ladies and I will pitch in to buy Jade back."

I return her tight smile. "Yep, and you'll just whet the appetite of a bunch of sharks. They taste blood and they'll be circling as long as we have a dollar in our coffers. No, ma'am, you'll not feed the beast. Leave that up to Tom, Colt, and our other gentlemen."

It's the first time I've crossed Miss Alice, and I can see in her eyes a mixture of anger and disappointment, but there are times you have to do what you think is right, in everyone's interest.

Alex pushes through the batwings, and without a hello asks, "What? I gotta town to watch over."

"We've got a lady gone missing, and have reason to believe the tong has her—"

He just shakes his head. "Another damn whore—"

"Not a dove, our laundry girl. A good young lady, a Chinese—"

"Case you don't know, we don't go into Chinatown... leave it to the Chinese."

He's parroting Miss Alice, and angering me, but I keep it to myself and finally say, "Thanks for dropping by," and he spins on his heel and is gone. It was all I could do not to say thanks for nothing.

Again I go to the rail and yell down to Dodge. "Put a sign out, we're closed today, but the crew is to come on in. Then when all are here, we have a meeting."

Again I get a shrug from Dodge, but he heads for the cellar stairs, I presume looking for some way to make a sign.

I return to my apartment with my Coach gun and revolver and recover my belly gun from my dresser, and check all their loads. I consider my Sharps but it's long, heavy, and not made for infighting so reject it.

As I'm waiting for my crew to arrive, I take the time to write my ma and assure her how much I love her and my sisters, and that with luck I'll see them early next year. I think, going into a potential shootout I'm assuring myself as much as my ma, but, of course, don't relay that to her. As I'm somewhat a man of means, I also write my will, copy it, return to my desk, and ask Alice to witness what I've written. I've found her to be a woman of her word and she promises to post it to my mother should my hide get ventilated beyond repair.

She tries again, "Jake, as I said, we can put together a thousand. All the ladies will pitch—"

"No, ma'am. Feeding the shark will only attract him back, and likely a whole school of them."

Only thirty minutes later I am surrounded by Colt Barberosa, Tennessee Tom, Abe, and our four dealers; Black Bob, a quiet-spoken Creole who seldom says more than "howdy" and "see ya," Freddy Hayes, Quinlon Cross, and Al "Cutter" MacGillicutty. They sit together on the gambling table side of the saloon. On the bar side, perched on stools, are our bartenders, Red Samuelson, Temple O'Toole, Dodge Filbertson and Flaco Comacho. Even our cook, Lars de Jong, stands by the door to his domain. I've just stepped up to present the task at hand, when to my pleased surprise, Obadiah Barnabas comes in through the balcony door to the bordello and walks to the railing.

"Howdy, how come you closed up shop? I had to come in the back way."

I yell up, "Glad you made it. Likely could use a hand."

As he descends the stairs, I turn to the others. "Fellas, we got a little problem. Seems some Chinese gents, the Gum San Tong they call themselves, think they can hold us up. Right now they want a thousand for the return of

Jade, one of our Chinee girls from next door. Some of you know her from the bath. Does anyone here think if we pay up that'll be the end of it?"

I scan them with a hard look. Get mostly shakes of the head and a couple of shrugs.

So I continue. "Well, next time it'll be five thousand and it could be another of our girls or even one of you or myself."

I still get no comment, so continue. "I think we gotta end this right now."

22

Flaco finally breaks their silence. "What about the coppers? Seems you befriend them every chance you get?"

"That's true, I do. But it also seems the tong does as well and maybe crosses some high placed palms with gold to leave them be. Looks like this is our problem to solve."

"And," Dodge asks, "how do you propose we solve it?"

Before I can answer, Tennessee Tom snaps, "With cudgels should that work, with lead if'n it takes more."

Freddy Portnoy, a dealer, who I've nicknamed "Daily," as every day he has a complaint, heads to his table, reaches to a shelf beneath where he's left his hat, centers it on his head, and says, over his shoulder, as he heads for the door, "Not me, I didn't sign on for no war where I'd likely get a tong hatchet split'n my noggin." He's a skinny fellow with shifty eyes and I've never trusted him.

"Hey," I yell after him, "you've got three days' pay coming."

He spins on a heel and heads back, when he's a couple

of paces away, I yell to Abe. "Mr. Abe, Freddy here wants to wait down below, locked in the storeroom until we return." The storeroom is windowless with a heavy door and brass padlock. Freddy's eyes flare knowing he's been tricked, but Abe and two others flank him so there's no running. And I add, "Won't do to have the tong know we're coming."

"You can't hold me," Freddy whines.

"Lock him up with a bottle of whatever he drinks."

'Hey, I'll go along—" he mumbles.

"Too late. Haul him down," I instruct, and Abe and Black Bob flank him and lead him to the stairway. I yell after him, "You'll be out come sunup. But you got the boot, so find other employment."

He yells over his shoulder, "Hey, a bottle of Sierra Shiner?"

"There's ten cases in the storeroom," I say, and they disappear with him. I turn back to my crew. "So, the rest of you gonna ride with the brand?"

Quinlon and Al MacGillicutty both look confused, and Al speaks up. "What's that mean?"

I forget I'm now with lots of city boys and brands are not common in the West. "That means we are together in solving this problem. Now, we don't have weapons for everyone?"

Nearly all of them reach under their coats, a couple into their boots, and Quinlon removes his short top hat and dang if he doesn't have a two-barrel derringer tucked up inside stowed in some sort of clips attached to the inside crown of the hat.

He's the only dealer I've worried about cheating since it was reported he was bottom dealing, but I've watched him close since. I now wonder if the derringer means he's worried about being caught? Then I shake it off. Far more than half the men in San Francisco, and most the women, go heeled. But I'll still watch him.

As I have no intention of approaching the tong head-quarters in the daylight, we have plenty of time. When Abe returns—I trusted him to return—I hand him a twenty-dollar gold piece. "Mr. Abe, head over to the nearest wheelwright and pick us up ten good hardwood spokes. The rest of you rest up, chow down but stay off the booze, use the privy. It may be a long night."

It's an interesting afternoon and evening. I have avoided getting to know the crew but as it seems as we are going into battle together, I take the time to go from table to table and engage them in conversation. They play cards, even some cribbage, in which I join. Temple climbs the stairs and mounts the piano stool—we'd moved it up to be near where Beth stationed herself near the rail to sing—and plays some lively tunes. I couldn't have been more surprised when Al MacGillicutty pulls out a mouth harp—a harmonica—and matches Temple song for song.

I do have a light moment as Tor, the hound, takes up the song and howls until Tom quiets him. His howl causes Mugsy to head for the small hole I've cut in my apartment door and disappear inside.

I'm pleased to learn that Dodge Filbertson sailed the Pacific and the China Sea, as I have, but he remained ashore long enough to learn some Mandarin so will have some use in this venture as an interpreter. If we do any talking.

We'd invested in a Seth Thomas wall clock, although Tom insisted it be kept up on the back wall well beyond the rail unseen from the saloon. He advised we didn't want those gambling or drinking to realize how late it was and head for home. Tricks of the trade I'm still learning. As quiet as it is without the crowd, we can hear it strike twelve.

I walk from man to man to check their weapons and make sure each have the first line of offense, a two-foot-long hardwood spoke, and we set out for the ten block hike. So as not to attract too much attention, we go in twos and threes. Abe and I lead, Colt and Tom follow at the rear, we keep at least a quarter block between comrades. It's a balmy evening for the bay city, with only a whisper of fog, so we are able to conceal the cudgels in the arms of coats. Strangely, holstered firearms and even carried long arms cause little notice. A group of men toting clubs would be another matter.

There're twelve of us, since Obey has joined in, taking imprisoned Freddy's place. We're two spokes short but Obey carries his whip, being a teamster a good part of the time. And he knows how to use it. I've seen him crack a cockroach off the barn wall without marking the wood. He offered to clip a button off'n my shirt, but I declined. Colt, too, has declined the use of a club, being far more comfortable with firearms. Temple, Abe, Tom, and I carry Coach guns.

I'm surprised Tom locks Tor away to keep him from following. I suggest he might be of help as he doesn't seem to take to our Celestial brothers. Tom assures me Tor's lack of fear might earn him a hatchet between his mournful eyes. And that would mean Tom wouldn't be happy until all Celestials were either cold in death or on their way back to their homeland…or both, as those who die in California lay aside money to be shipped home for burial.

As we turn into what's becoming known as China-town, I'm surprised that it's lit far better than the streets we approached via, lots of lanterns, some permanent ones on poles, many paper ones in windows. And a few shops still open, so their lanterns are burning. There are few still on the street, and no ladies. I'm walking with Colt and Tom, the others follow in twos and threes. We approach the tong headquarters on both sides of the street. Unlike a few near the center of town, this street is not planked but dirt, and fairly muddy as the San Francisco nights are fogbound, thus nearly always moist.

I'm concerned when I see a group of four men on their haunches, one of whom is studying us with what I consider too much interest, then I realize they are passing an opium pipe around. They are so far-gone they wouldn't flinch if we were a herd of grizzly bears.

We pull up a couple of shops short of the three-story brick building that's the Gum San Tong. I can see the ground floor is a shop of some kind but can't read the Chinese characters that are its sign and am not yet close enough to see in the glass pane in the door.

We've stopped near a passageway between buildings and Tom suggests, "We don't want anyone fleeing out the back...particularly if they're dragging Jade along. He waves Black Bob and Quinlon up. "We're going in the back way," he instructs, and they move quietly away.

I call after him, "Don't be shootin' anyone less'n they've got a long braid."

He waves over his shoulder.

I give them time to reach the alley and make the turn toward our target, then move forward, waving the others up. The front of the building is set ten feet back from the boardwalk, and the stone stepping-stones leading to the door are lined with some kind of low-flowering shrub and flanked by two twice-life-size Chinese stone dogs, that most would think are lions.

I shush our fellows with a finger to my lips and

motion for them to stay on the boardwalk, and move forward, up a couple of steps, and try the door.

Locked.

So I peek in one of the four one foot by one foot panes of glass in the door. And see it's an herb shop the Chinee folks are famous for. Not only do bunches of greenery and dried things hang in profusion, but dried critters, snakes, and frogs, and such hang along the far wall. Then I see there are also cages which I presume hold live critters. One wall is shelves from floor to ceiling with over a hundred glass and crockery containers, each with a label.

There is one candle burning at the back of the shop, on a desk, and at the desk is a man with pen in hand, dipping it into an inkwell. I turn and motion for my mates to move to the side so as to be out of sight, then rap on the door. He glances up, then returns to his task. So I rap a little more insistently.

He looks up, the irritation plain on dark eyes over a nearly white mustache and beard. He arranges the cap on his head then rises and heads for the door. It comes to me that if his shelves and bottles are medicines, it's not unlikely he'd have customers at all hours. Then again, I see a shelf full of opium pipes and the small bottles normally containing the narcotic. My interest is not in his happy-smoke—which I've come to think of as poison smoke as I've seen fine men rot with its use—his medicines, or snakes and toads, but rather in the stairway on the southside of the shop, leading up.

He opens the door and is a little shocked when I drag him outside. He starts to yell but I cover his mouth with a hand. He's an old man or I would have lollygagged him up aside the head with my spoke.

Dodge steps forward and takes the old man by the

arm, mutters something to him, and the old fellow strides off down the street as spry as if only twelve years old.

I look at Dodge questioningly, and he offers, "Told him we'd cut off his queue if he didn't run for the hills. Can't get into heaven without your braid. He said more than half dozen of his chums and the girls are upstairs. Girls on the very top."

"Let's get this done," I reply, and head for the stairway.

23

GIVING HIM A SMILE AND A NOD, I WHISPER TO THE others. "Let's get Jade," and head up the stairway. I shouldn't be surprised to see a heavy door at the top of the stairs. I am surprised to reach for the knob and have it open just before I lay a hand on it.

I'm no more surprised than is the huge man now standing in the open doorway. He grunts, his eyes narrow as he tries to make out who's in the dark stairwell.

I don't give him time to focus, and with one step bring the spoke's fat end down on the crown of his head hard enough to fell a mule…but he merely staggers back, giving me time to flank him and shove him forward.

Colt, Al "Cutter" MacGillicutty, and Flaco Comacho are nearest me following up the stairs, and I see spokes fly as the huge man—he's far shorter than myself but as round as he is tall—is now running the gantlet as he tumbles down the stairs. Our men have to flatten themselves against the walls to keep from being swept down the stairs with him, but they manage to get in a few more blows as he passes. He lands like a beached whale, unmoving.

I'm startled as I turn back to make more progress, by men pouring out of the shadows, then take a deep breath as I realize it's Tom, Black Bob, and Quinlon topping another stairway coming up from the alley. We're in what appears to be a landing with a stairway leading down to the shop in the front, one down to the alley in the back, and with three doors leading front, back, and side. The stairway in the back is topped with another stairway leading up to the third floor. The side door has light leaking through a crack at the bottom.

The ruckus of the big man playing the bowling ball is bound to have raised attention. We're standing as quietly as a dozen men possibly could, when we hear footsteps of more than one man through the side door. I rush forward and flank the door, as Tom and Colt step into my place.

Three men, the first at least as tall as me, fly out the side door as light fills the landing. I wait until the third one passes then step forward and put the cudgel to work. He hits the floor like I've dropped a hundred-pound sack of flour, but another man is behind them and swings a hatchet and I feel it bury in my heavy coat—and thank God for the heavy coat as he tries to recover it but it's hung up in the wool.

The roar of a Coach gun shatters the sounds of the scuffle and one of the two that passed me spins past the other way and bounces off the wall and hits the floor in a bloody heap. Then the sharp report of a revolver is followed by another shotgun blast. It's far too tight a space for a gun battle. As soon as the echo quiets Tom yells at me.

"They're still coming," and I turn back to the open

door. This time I raise my Coach gun but see two men turn and run, their queues flopping in the air behind. I step into the room just in time to see them jumping out two windows in the rear of the thirty-foot-deep room. Two more doors lead off the big room to the side. With Tom and Colt close behind, I head for the door nearest the street. It's locked so I apply a boot with my full weight behind and it flies open, it's hasp and trim shattered.

Again, I'm just in time to see the back of a man's white shirt disappear out the window.

No one else in the room.

I get back into the main room just in time to see Colt and Tom prepare to kick in the second door, luckily they stand to the side as someone inside fans a revolver and holes pepper the door. The rest of our crew has crowed into the room, and I see Al MacGillicutty spin and go to the floor. Both Colt and Tom have dropped to a knee and both fire a barrel of a Coach gun into the room.

"He's done," Tom shouts, then eyeballing the room, shouts again, "All clear."

"Then up another floor," I yell, and head back to the landing and for the stairway to the third. Black Bob and Quinlon are ahead of me and reach the foot of the third-floor stairway just in time to meet two tong members coming down, both with revolvers still stuffed in their sashes, but with hatchets in hand. They don't make it to the foot of the stairs still standing.

I've never heard gunfire in so close a space, and my ears are ringing so loudly I hope I can hear any yelled warnings.

Bob and Quin step over the bodies and head up the stairs ahead of me. I see not a door but a door-size set of bars at the top, with a chain hanging and a large, but open, padlock.

As Bob passes through the door, the high-toned screams of a bevy of women ring out. I follow Quin into the room which is entirely open, but two dozen cots are spaced throughout and an equal number of women are gathered at the rear of the room, pressed tightly together as if being in a mass would protect them.

"Jade!" I yell.

Almost as quickly I hear the reply, "Jake Zane san," and she steps out of the group and runs to me and throws her arms around me.

"Let's get the hell out of here," Tom says, "before they bring an army down on us."

"We're taking them all," I snap.

"Foolish," Tom says.

"Can't leave them," Colt concurs.

So I instruct Jade, "They can bring what they can carry, but we go now!" and I guess I say "now" and little loudly as she flinches, but she's understood, and yells at the other girls and they head for the stairway.

Al is conscious but bleeding from a hole in his side, hopefully through and through, and is helped to his feet with an arm over the shoulders of both Abe and Red Samuelson.

We hit the street below with two dozen Chinee girls, all in their nightgowns, but all seeming to be very happy to flee the barracoon.

As soon as we turn off Dupont, clearing Chinatown, I yell at Flaco who trots up beside me. I think he's the most agile, and probably the youngest of us, and instruct him to run ahead, and I mean run, and fetch Dr. Southerby. The doctor's home over office is only two blocks from The Piccadilly, and instruct him to ask the doctor to meet us there.

We're a parade working our way to safety, and I note we're followed by two large Chinamen, each with a hatchet tucked into their sashes. But they keep their distance.

We reach The Piccadilly without incident.

And only then do I realize, what the devil am I going to do with a couple of dozen Chinee girls? And, to add possible injury to insult, the tong knows where they've been taken.

Then I remember, I'd faced this dilemma before, when I'd helped recover the sister of my dear friend who was a Kanaka, a Sandwich Islander. But then we'd had Lady Stanley-Smyth who came to their rescue.

As I recall, she was a benefactor of some young lady's school in Sacramento. But two dozen? It seems a lot to ask of any institution. And the lady no longer can help us.

I decide, as the shivers ware off from having lead fly all around me, and digging a hatchet out of the thick wool of my coat, that I'll conjure on it after a good night's sleep.

Alice meets us at the door of the saloon, and immediately grabs me by the shoulders, "Your trousers are covered with blood."

I guess the hatchet did find a little meat.

24

Dr. Southerby is not yet on the scene. We lay Al on a faro table and Tom and Colt go about tending his wound. It seems the two shootists have some experience with gunshots.

Miss Alice leads me up to my quarters, yells at Jade and her ma, Lily, who's still sobbing and thanking all of us for the return of her daughter, to fetch hot water and clean cloths. She seats me on one of two ladder-back chairs in my apartment and helps me remove my coat and, I now see, bloodied shirt. The hatchet has carved a cut only three inches long and a quarter inch deep across my bottom rib on the left side, not even deep enough to put Miss Alice's sewing skills to test. I have a bottle of brandy on the little chest of drawers holding my white bowl and pitcher and shaving gear, a strop hangs at its side, and she grabs the bottle. I think I'm getting a swig, but she spreads the cut and splashes it on. It won't do to yelp like a kicked cur, so I grin a little stupidly rather than cry out and bear it without much more than a flinch. But I'm yelling inside.

Mugsy is watching from a box near the door to my deck and jumps up and leaps onto the bed and snuggles up to my side. It seems she knows I'm slightly injured.

In moments, I'm wrapped in a clean bandage and invited down to a celebration in the saloon.

Dr. Southerby has arrived, and Al is not so quiet as I forced myself to be as the doctor runs a swab soaked in alcohol clean through the wound—through and through his side. In fact, Al screams like a scalded cat, and I'm not alone in having to wince and close my eyes.

The doctor glances over at me as I near, and as soon as he can be heard over Al's caterwauling comments, he says, "He'll be fine, so long as it didn't clip a bowel or doesn't go green."

As Alice is near, I instruct her, "Please, put a cot in my living area so I can watch over him."

She nods, waves Abe to help, and disappears up the stairs. I remember the two tong boys following, so decide caution is called for. I ask Temple and Red if they'll take up a position on the second floor of the brothel, the best place to watch the street for approaching enemies. They take a couple of Coach guns and I hear them agreeing to trade watches through the night.

The unmarried of our crew, a half dozen strong, agree to spend the night just in case we have more trouble. Lily and Jade fetch bedding and our saloon floor, bar, and faro tables become sleeping facilities.

We're just about to bed down, and me to join Al in my quarters, when Tom appears at the rail above, and shouts down, "A half-dozen coppers about to bang on the door."

I sigh deeply.

The bang on the door is more than insistent, in fact it sounds a little more like a battering ram.

I stride and open the batwings and unlock and open the heavy doors and am shoved aside as seven coppers shove their way in, each with a revolver in one hand and long nightstick in the other. I'm sorry to note that I don't know any of them.

"Who's the boss man here?" A barrel-chested copper snaps.

"I'll do," I say.

"And who might you be, boyo?" He steps near and shoves the end of his nightstick into my chest.

"I'm Jake Zane, Lord Stanley-Smyth's representative. And you'll keep that prod to yourself if you don't want it to find a spot behind you where the sun don't shine."

He guffaws. "I guess you want it to land between your eyes." Then adds, "Lord Stanley-Smyth? I've only got one lord, youngster, and it sure as hell's hot not some bloody Englishman. You're all, and I mean all…dealers, bartenders, swampers, and whores, under arrest."

I eye him a little incredulously, "What the hell for?"

"As if you don't know," he snaps. His men have fanned out, and all are fanning the room with their revolvers.

"You best have a chat with Willowby before you disturb the peace of this establishment."

He stares at me a moment, so I add, "And Mayor Chastine and Judge Hoffman. I believe their opinion trumps that of a bunch of heathen Chinamen who I'm sure cross your palms with silver—"

"Watch it, boyo."

"I don't make idle chitchat, boyo," I give it right back to him, and glance up at the railing above and am taken aback to see the railing lined with our ladies from next door, and each of them is yielding a firearm. And Tor is behind Tom, looking as if he's about to go for the copper's throat.

Alice shouts down, "And, you, you squinty-eyed son of a bitch, all those he mentioned are customers of ours, as are half the men you've dragged in behind you. If you don't turn tail and get the hell out of The Piccadilly and Miss Alice's Pleasure Parlour, each and every one of those of us of the fairer sex will call upon the fairer sex of those you love and cherish and describe to them every wart and scar on your skinny butts, features only a woman who has intimate knowledge would have knowledge of. Along with how much of the household money...and I keep good records...you've traded for tokens."

I can't help but smile. Then laugh. Then add, "I've always heard a little knowledge can be dangerous. Unless y'all want to have wives with crossed legs and cold suppers waiting the end of your shifts, I'd suggest you arrange to have a meeting with myself, yourself, and Marshal Willowby some comfortable time of the morning. Invite the mayor and the judge should you see fit."

As I'm speaking, all the coppers are sheepishly fading back toward the door.

I believe we've won this round. Sometimes gall is a good weapon.

The barrel-chested copper yells just before he shuts the door behind himself, "This ain't over."

And I return the yell, "See you at ten in the morning."

As soon as he shuts the door, all of us turn to the railing, doff our hats, and bow at the dozen ladies lining the railing above.

They laugh and head back next door.

I sleep fitfully, even knowing Tom and Colt are

standing guard. The cut on my side awakens me each time I roll over, and the occasional moan of Al in the next-door room causes concern and I listen each time, expecting him to call out for something.

Lars and Emma, our cooks, have outdone themselves, sending out for sweetbreads, cooking up an omelet that fills a two-foot diameter camp skillet, frying up side pork from half a hog, and slathering biscuits with gravy, so the crew and I are well-fed. Alice, Jade, and Dodge accompany me to Marshal Willowby's office and we arrive promptly at ten a.m.

Two large Chinamen with hatchets in sashes are near the street door, but we pass without giving them much more than a glance, even though they place hands on hatchet handles as we near.

Maybe my hand on my holstered revolver gives them pause.

25

I'M ONLY A LITTLE SURPRISED WHEN ENTERING Willowby's private office to see two Chinese gentlemen present, as well as Willowby and his secretary, seated with pen and inkwell. One of the Chinese is dressed in the long knee-length shirt and has the normal queue hanging to his waist. He's as gray as the other, but the other has hair cut like a banker and an expensive suit and four-in-hand silk tie. Had it not been for hair as black as a raven's wing and skin the color of our cooks' turmeric, he could be taken for an English banker. And his speech is as proper.

He addresses Willowby without bothering with a hello. "These are the people who broke into our property, killed two of our members, wounded two more, and kidnapped a dozen of our ladies?" He gets no immediate reply, so adds, "You punish them, or we will."

I don't give Willowby chance to answer, as the heat floods my backbone. "You mean punish those who rescued our lady and freed slaves which are illegal in

California. I don't lie and I won't tolerate lies and liars. And if you say you didn't hold our lady and lots of others to be sold as slaves, you're a liar."

Willowby, palms out flat cautioning both of us, speaks up. "I'll hear both sides. Zane, this is Yi Wong, spokesman for most those on Dupont Street. Wong, I guess you know this is Jake Zane, from The Piccadilly."

Neither of us extends a hand to shake. So I address my comments to Willowby, "I've brought Miss Jade, who was kidnapped and held by this man's tong. Do you want to hear from her? I have a couple of dozen more Chinese ladies who I'm sure would be happy to tell their stories."

Again it's the well-dressed Chinese who speaks up, and takes a step nearer me, and he's as tall and broad shouldered as I am. As he does, he points at Miss Alice and Jade, but he's looking with eyes as black as night at me. "You bring a woman to men's work. So I presume you are a woman yourself or need to hide behind the skirts of one."

That takes me back a step, and I'm afraid I'm so astounded I mutter, with fists balled at my sides. "Wo… Wong, do you see a skirt on me. I'll be happy to show you what a man I am."

"You have called us liars. If you are a man you will accept our challenge to duel. I will select one of our kinsmen…"

That takes me back a moment, and Willowby's mouth drops open. Finally I say, "You have made the challenge, so I choose the weapons, and it's not swords or hatchets, it's revolvers and not at ten paces. It's fifty feet where I can notch your or your 'kinsmens" ears if need be. Maybe both if you're nearby. And my lead travels faster that even a well-throwns hatchet."

Mister suit and tie is equally silent as I stand, the answer to his challenge hanging in the air. But Willowby is not. "Gentlemen, there will be no duel. If you want to fight it out, it will be in the courtroom." Then he steps closer to mister suit and tie, and adds, "And there will be witnesses and a judge. Are you sure you want an abolitionist judge originally from New Hampshire, who authored California's laws against slavery to judge the keeping and selling of slaves?"

But mister suit is not about to give up. "It's a common practice in China, and—"

Willowby stops him short. "You're not in China, Mr. Wong, you're in California and California is not a slave state."

"They have killed two and wounded—"

Again Willowby stops him. "Killed two kidnappers, two slave masters. Were I you, Mr. Wong, I'd return to Chinatown and call it a day before half of San Francisco decides it's Chinese moving day and runs every man with a queue out of the city."

"Sir," Wong says, and his tone is ominous, "there would be a war."

So I add, "And the streets would be littered with Chinese bodies. I don't want to see that, and you don't want to see that. I have trusted and respected Chinese in my employ and want them to enjoy the same rights as the rest of us. However, there's an old adage, Mr. Wong, and that's: 'When in Rome do as the Romans do.' You're in the newest state of the United States and all of America is watching how California conducts herself, so California is a free state and all who are here are freemen…and women…and all of California, including the United States Army at the Presidio, will stand against slavery. If you want to trade in slaves, I suggest you travel to Texas or Louisiana or other parts south where the devilish practice is accepted."

Wong is silent for a moment, then spins on his heel and heads for the door, letting his silent associate exit first. He turns back and again his tone is ominous. "Willowby, your people took our money—"

Willowby raises his voice, "If you want to file a complaint against some of my people, the court will entertain it. I took no money from anyone, and I'll not book your saying so. Know one thing, Wong, your people want their bodies sent back to China should they die here. You start a war and so many will be packed in salt and charcoal, the tongs will pay for a half-dozen full-rigged ships to cross the Pacific."

Wong bites his tongue, merely nodding, and closes Willowby's door.

As soon as they're gone, I turn to Willowby. "Thank you, sir."

"You're welcome, so long as this affair came down as you say it did. And you should know, if money has changed hands in Chinatown, it hasn't crossed my palm."

"Never thought it might have," I say.

He turns to Miss Alice, Dodge, and Jade. "And you three understand no money crossed my palm?" Both Dodge and Miss Alice nod, but Jade obviously doesn't understand. Dodge tries to get the point across but still she shrugs.

"Doesn't matter," Willowby says, then adds, "if you have any trouble with the tongs, try and let my office handle it. Thanks for coming in."

And we head back to The Piccadilly.

We only get a block before I realize the two Chinese

who were near the door when we entered are staying a half block behind, so I spin on my heel and start back.

"What?" Miss Alice calls after me, but I'm striding forward. They let me get within thirty feet before they spin on their heel and begin to jog away.

I yell after them, "You dog my trail and I shoot you down like curs," but have no idea if they understand. I'm sure they do understand I have a hand on my revolver.

Hopefully, it's the last I see of them.

And, shortly after we return to the shop it is Chinese moving day, but not the kind the goldfields are famous for. Miss Alice, Colt, and I herd the two dozen ladies from the barracoon away from their temporary home at The Piccadilly down to the waterfront. All of us load up on the steamer *McKim* for a seventeen-hour voyage upriver to Sacramento City. At over three hundred tons, the *McKim* has plenty of room for us. Of course, at the rate of twenty-five dollars a head she should have luxury accommodations. We still suffer from goldfield prices, of course The Piccadilly profits from goldfield prices so I shouldn't complain.

Miss Alice books herself a stateroom for an additional ten dollars.

I have no idea if this endeavor is something of which Lord Stanley-Smyth would approve, so I leave an IOU in Victor, the safe, for the six hundred dollars I borrow for the ladies' passage. Now having over two thousand dollars in savings, I could pay for it myself, and Miss Alice has offered one thousand to help. The fact is this whole thing came about due to a Piccadilly employee being kidnapped, which wouldn't have happened had the tong not believed the very successful saloon and bawdy house could pay. I can only hope Lord Stanley-Smyth sees it my way and tears up my note.

I wonder how I will raise the two thousand four hundred dollars, one hundred each, for the tuition to the English Standard School for Young Ladies for a single six-month session. Where we are bound.

26

I'M FACING THE EXORBITANT SUM OF TWO THOUSAND FOUR hundred dollars to enroll the ladies, and that's just for one half this school year but includes room and board for the next six months...and of course is contingent upon the acceptance of nearly as many Chinese ladies as are students already enrolled. The hope is as the school has a half-dozen young women from the Sandwich Islands as students, Chinese will not be so much of a stretch.

I'll soon know. God knows I can't afford the trip back to San Francisco hauling two dozen rejected ladies, as for some unknown reason the return trip is thirty dollars a head. And that with the current?

We're overnight on the *McKim*, happy that we're with some tough ladies who've survived a trip across the Atlantic, only to be forced up the stairs of a barracoon to await being auctioned off to the highest bidder. As uncomfortable as the hardwood decks of the *McKim* are, I guess they're better than being a slave. By midmorning we'll have completed the four-mile hike from the docks of Sacramento City to the school, and I'll know if our trip is for naught.

Miss Alice, after a night in her stateroom, is fresh as the proverbial daisy while I feel, after sleeping the night away on the deck and keeping my eye out for those who might have some illegitimate interest in our young ladies, feel like I've been rowing against the current from San Francisco to Sacramento City. Dodge seems no better. As he has a smattering of the language, it's been Dodge who's escorted the ladies to the boat's privy when any of the two dozen had the urge.

But we're securely docked, and the gangway awaits.

I'm a little surprised to see how Sacramento City has grown since I was last here over two years ago. The streets are planked and a variety of shops are now brick, as only a year ago most of the city burned. Sacramento is vying to become the capitol of California and to take that honor away from Benicia, which we passed on our larboard, or port, on the way upriver. And I can see why they think they deserve the honor as Sacramento City is five times the size of Benicia and on the confluence of two of the state's major rivers, the Sacramento after which the city was named, and the American. Both rivers serve as major arteries feeding supplies to and taking riches from the state's major source of both fame and income, the goldfields.

We make quite a parade, Miss Alice leading the way in a rented buggy, two dozen Celestial ladies walking mostly two by two following, Dodge and myself taking up the rear. We attract a lot of attention and a few comments as we pass through town. The school is four miles up the American River and after asking directions am told to look for a large two-story white structure with Grecian columns atop a hill, with corrals, a small orchard and barn, as well as a long swingle-story building which serves as dormitory for the students.

It appears they've seen us coming as a gentleman of generous girth, a shock of white hair, a matching handlebar mustache, four-in-hand red silk tie, fully dressed in a dark suit and brocaded waistcoat, awaits on the porch. Only slightly at his rear is a dark-skinned lady in a flowered dress to her ankles. It seems they eat well as she two is buxom and barrel shaped.

He steps forward and helps Miss Alice from the carriage.

"Madam, you've driven yourself," he says, with a deep resonant voice.

She smiles and nods. "Miss Alice Deschamps, and you are?"

"Colonel Harrison Hargrave, master of the English Standard School for Young Ladies at your service, Miss Deschamps. And this is my wife, Melana, and head-mistress. And what do we have here?" He waves a hand at the ladies as Dodge and I close the distance.

I've heard the English accent from many a sailor, and his is the same, if more refined.

As his wife, who we learn is Polynesian from the Sandwich Islands, shows the girls around, the colonel, Miss Alice, Dodge, and myself are seated at a dining room table in the main house, explaining the situation and negotiating the education and housing of the girls. Hargrave explains the girls are four to a room in ten rooms in the long single-story building behind the main structure, which serves as the Hargraves' home and school, with living quarters on the top floor for him and his wife, classrooms, kitchen, and dining room on the lower.

After spending a great deal of time convincing

Colonel Hargrave he should accept so many Celestial girls—he complains he doesn't want the school to be known as the Chinese Standard School for Young Ladies. However, as Lady Stanley-Smyth has been a supporter, he's making an exception. I find myself signing a note for two thousand four hundred dollars, the largest financial transaction in my life, for the first six-month sessions for the girls. I'm obligated to pay four hundred dollars per month, I do manage to get him to waive interest so long as my payments are on time. I do manage to convince him to accept the postmark as "on time," and not the arrival of the draft. Miss Alice assures me she'll help raise money to cover the note as the payments will quickly delete my savings. In addition, Miss Alice will remain as a guest overnight, but as part of our deal Dodge and I will stay on the week it will take the two of us and the school's handyman, a former slave called Leo, to convert the attic of the main building to a dorm for fourteen of the girls. The other ten will be accommodated by adding a cot to each of the ten rooms. The girls will be expected to help with the large garden and orchard—plums, peaches, figs, apricots, and black walnuts—plus chickens, ducks, geese, pigeons, rabbits, pigs, sheep, four milk cows, and a pond stocked with trout and catfish, all of which is part of their education. Of course many of them were farm girls in China, and the Hargraves may be the students in some instances.

I had not planned to be away from The Piccadilly for more than two days, and, with the morning, make a quick trip into town driving Miss Alice and making sure she's safely aboard a side-wheeler for the trip downriver. Again, it's shank's mare back to the school and soon I have hammer in hand. The attic has eight dormer windows, four front and back, which lends itself to eight rooms, so will house two more than required at two to the room. As the colonel had made plans to construct more dorm rooms in the rear, he has milled lumber. In only four days we have finished all but hanging doors, a task Leo can easily accomplish alone. The colonel releases Dodge and me and we are able to catch the evening boat downriver. Tired, blistered hands, but with a feeling of accomplishment, we return.

Now, all I have to do is figure how to make the payments on the note. I'm thinking it will be easy until, midmorning, we hoof it from the waterfront to The Piccadilly...and find the front of the bordello and saloon burned with only a few charred sticks standing.

What the hell happened?

Tennessee Tom is inside directing the cleanup. On closer inspection I see it's only the front of the bordello that's totally destroyed. It's eaten into the front of the saloon about ten feet, the corner nearest the bordello. The main doors and batwings are still standing, as well as the paned windows next to them, and the sign. Strangely the boardwalk in front of our saloon doors is burned. Tom now has a three-wide two by six walkway from the plank street to the batwings.

I wind my way through a half-dozen workers who are sweeping and sawing. Already there's a lift of milled lumber on hand for rough repairs.

"What the hell happened?" I ask Tom.

"The night you left. The son of a bitch who did it left a can out in the street. Coal oil. Lucky the Foggy Town Fire Brigade was returning from putting out a grass fire up on Nob Hill, had just refilled their tank, or we might have lost half the town again."

"Any idea who?" I ask.

"Your guess is good as mine. You were leaving with

some substantial assets of the Gum San Tong, on the hoof but assets...then again maybe our soiled dove murderer has stepped up his game and decided, why kill one at a time when he can kill them all with a can of coal oil."

I weigh the possibilities for a moment. Then suggest, "Then again maybe that crazy lout who calls himself Elohim, God, and thinks he's doing God's work...as if any of us knows such. Or more likely the tong." Then, shrugging, "So, maybe it's time to call on the tong again, only this time to wipe them out."

"Abe is over on Dupont seeing what the talk is. If the tong did it, it's likely they're crowing about it."

"When are we back in business?" I ask.

"Hell, I'm gonna cover us up with tent canvas and we're building a walkway across the burned-out board-walk...soon as I get more lumber. I say open her up tomorrow night."

"And Miss Alice's establishment?"

"That'll take more time. You take a look, but I say we cut the front ten feet off. We'll lose a couple of rooms topside and part of the salon, but back in business in a week at most."

I sigh deeply. I'm not as far behind the eight ball as I'd feared.

Just as we finish our conversation, Abe pushes his way through the madhouse that's a dozen men cutting away fire damage. Four work with a pair of eight-foot crosscut saws as if they're felling redwoods, and sawdust flies.

"Welcome home," I greet Abe, and get a nod in return, so I continue, "so, what did you learn?"

"Seems they're gloating a mite, saying it serves The Piccadilly right, but no one on Dupont is bragging about burning us out. A couple of fellas was saying they wished it was them..."

I turn back to Tom. "Have we had a count of our ladies?"

Just as he's about to answer, he instead points at Miss Alice who's hurrying up.

"More trouble?" I ask before she can speak.

"None of the girls were hurt in the fire. Some still coughing from the smoke is all. All got out the back way. But Juliet, who was first out, has not returned. She's now gone more than forty-eight hours."

"No one saw anything suspicious?" I ask. Juliet, a waif whose age I questioned. She claimed twenty-one but looked sixteen to me. Alice didn't seem to mind, but I thought it criminal if she was truly so young. I could have been influenced by her height, as she was short of five feet, I'd guess only four feet, nine inches. I couldn't help but feel the men who asked for her feared full-grown women or had a perversion for children. All that said, she was beautiful, a small beautiful jewel.

"Goldy was next out and saw what she thought was a delivery wagon disappearing down the alley. She didn't think anything of it until the girls realized Juliet was missing."

"She wasn't unhappy...didn't just run off?"

"I have four hundred plus dollars of her money among the girls' savings in Victor. She wouldn't just run off and leave her hard-earned."

So I turn back to Abe. "Can you head over to the marshal's office and ask Sergeant Alex O'Toole to stop by."

"Yessur," he says, and spins on a heel and is gone. I turn back to Alice. "And where's Beth?"

"She hired the pianist from the Metropolitan and

she's there rehearsing. Al's to return and escort her back at four this afternoon."

With all the madness of Celestial ladies to Sacramento and discovering the calamity of the fire on my return, I'd forgotten Beth's concert is only two days away.

I inquire, "Did the flyers arrive from the printer? I should have had them up days ago."

"They did and Abe, Beth, and I took care posting them. The box office at the Met has sold half the seats."

I don't say it but am happy to hear that news as it means I'll get most, if not all, my money back. Seems with the new circumstance of becoming a benefactor of a bevy of young ladies' education, finances are suddenly a major worry. Seems all the ladies, other than Juliet, are accounted for…but come to think of it, not all—I haven't seen Mugsy. I've carried a small backpack to Sacramento so use the time awaiting Alex to return to my little apartment and stow my personals. I'm pleased to awaken Mugsy, who's sprawled on my bed. She rises, arches her back in a feline stretch, then jumps down, trots over, and rubs against my leg as I'm putting my things in my small chest of drawers. I give her ears a scratch and head back to the saloon floor. I'm pleased to see Alex bellied up to the bar.

As I shake hands, I ask, "I don't suppose you've had any word about our lady, Juliet?"

He gives me a disgusted glance. "Damnable whores cause us more trouble than the sailors and miners. She likely ran off with some lucky digger whose pockets bulge with nuggets."

"If so, she left her earnings in the safe. A good amount so I'm told."

Alex shrugs. "If she don't show up you can give it over to our widows and orphans fund."

I'm a little taken aback by that, and by his attitude, so add, "If she doesn't have next of kin on file, we might do that."

"Might?"

"We'll do what we think is right."

"Humph," he says, and changes the subject by eyeing the work going on. "You're moving right along."

"We need to get open and it's important we have some security other than canvas. Some owlhoot could break in with a penknife."

"I'll double the patrols. You're normally open till three and the sun's up at six or so. You'll be fine."

"Appreciate the extra patrols." I shake again. "I've got several days of take to count up."

He's quiet for a moment. "How much you keep in that big Victor safe?"

I find that a bit of a strange question, but answer, "Most goes straight away to Adams or a couple of banks we now deal with. My blessed ma taught me not to keep all my eggs in one basket."

"Clever lady, your ma."

"Back to work," I say, and head for the stairs. I yell at Tom to join me at my table, then send Abe next door to beckon Miss Alice. Colt is left to watch the progress of our carpenters.

With no one making a run to Adams, I soon discover we have over five thousand dollars to place in the safe and have over seven thousand there. We pay our vendors cash from the till, placing receipts in place of the coin expended so the drawers should balance at closing. The cash on hand, after paying the help, is nearly all pure profit. And it's a good thing, as the repairs will exceed two thousand dollars.

As the day wears on I see Abe returning with Beth. She's radiant...in fact resplendent...in a new yellow gown with matching parasol, and I hurry over to greet her, only to get a tight smile and nod of the head as she passes. She gives me her back and I call after her, "How was the rehearsal?"

She waves over her shoulder and calls out over the hammering and sawing. "Fine." And that's it. Ma said I should never expect to understand the ladies, and boy oh boy is she proving right again.

28

MAYBE IT'S CURIOSITY BUT AS THE EVENING WEARS ON WE have one of the biggest crowds since our grand opening. I get lots of compliments as to the rapid progress being made but refer them to Tennessee Tom as it's his hard work that got things going while I was caring for the Celestial ladies.

As the witching hour nears, I wave Abe and Colt over. "How about you two grabbing some shut-eye until closing time. I wanna post guards front and back as we're doing business in a damn tent."

Colt shrugs. "Hell, ol' Victor must weigh five hundred—"

"Seven hundred pounds," I correct.

"And clumsy as hell. Take ten men to lug him out."

I give him a knowing smile, and ask, "I do believe there are more than ten steal-anything-not-bolted-down dirty thieves in San Francisco, don't you?"

He smiles a little sheepishly. "I do believe ten times that amount. I'll borrow some bedding from Miss Alice and make me a pad behind the bar."

Abe grunts, and adds, "And I'll take me a chair up on the balcony with a Coach gun, should that please you, Mr. Zane. I gots no trouble staying awake till Mr. Sun peeks over the East."

"Pleased as a wolf caught him a fat rabbit," I reply, giving him a nod.

I really don't expect trouble, but better prepared than caught unaware.

As I lock the big doors behind the batwings, I have to smile as only fifteen feet away is nothing but open framing and canvas cover. As I said, a penknife would give access with a quick sweep. Tomorrow the wood siding goes up and we'll be secure again. That said, the whole front of the bordello is canvas over studs spaced two feet apart. And a robber could slip in the bordello, climb the stairs, and find himself on the saloon balcony.

But all we have to do is get through a few hours tonight, then we should be safe again.

I'm nearly in dreamland when my eyes snap open. Something is amiss, then I realize there's a gentle tapping on my door. This is not an urgent tapping, but a gentle tap, tap, tap, a pause, then three taps.

I rise, pull on my trousers and suspenders over a bare chest, shove my Colt Sheriff's Model into my waistband at my back, and, in stocking feet, stand to the side of the door.

"What's up?" I question, without flipping up the latch I've taken to using.

"Can't sleep," comes back a lady voice, sultry, in not much more than a whisper.

Had I known who it was, I'd have slipped on my shirt.

Beth, wide-eyed, hair piled atop her head, in a silk robe over her nightshirt—or so I suppose.

I'm a little taken aback, needless to say. I stand staring, then mumble, "Should I get a shirt."

"I had a daddy, you know. I've seen a hairy chest. You gonna invite me in or leave me in the hall like a washerwoman coming to gather up the laundry?"

I swing the door wide and step aside.

She walks in and her eyes sweep the room. "No bed?"

I find that a salacious question, considering the circumstance, but only point. "Through that door."

"My goodness, you have fancy commodious accommodations." I've noticed she often uses two-dollar words, wondering if I understand. And I as often thank my ma for testing me far more often.

"And a privy out on the deck. Room for half the crew," I say.

"May I sit?" she asks.

"I'm so sorry. I'm rude. Fact is surprise has taken my breath and I guess my manners."

She laughs, a sweet lilting sound. "You've never had a lady call on you...and you a few steps from a dozen of the city's most beautiful sporting ladies?"

"Lord Stanley-Smyth advised me a man shouldn't take advantage of ladies in his employ. I believe his words were, and I quote, 'unseemly and unsporting,' an unfair advantage in waging the war of love. He then laughed so I wonder if he was serious...about love being a war, I mean." I shrug, giving her a chance to reply, but she merely bats her long lashes, so then I continue. "I guess normally it would be me doing the calling. You barely spoke this afternoon. I figured you mad at me?"

"Jake Zane, should I get angry with you, you'll not have to figure on it. I had some trouble with my contralto and was upset. Should I get angry with you, you'll know it straight away."

157

"So," I say, purposely looking worried, "your contralto was broken."

She laughs. "Just couldn't quite get low enough."

She closes the three steps between us, and to my astonishment, throws her arms around my neck, goes up on her toes, and just as her lips touch mine, the roar of what I suppose is both barrels of a twelve-gauge shotgun rattles the room, and my backbone even more than the near kiss has. Rattles so hard dust motes float down from the ceiling.

As much as I was enjoying her warm breath on my lips, her obviously unbound breasts against my bare chest, I shove her away. Grabbing my own scatter-gun in one hand, I palm the Colt in the other, and charge out the door.

I yell over my shoulder. "Lock the door and stay low."

"Jake!" I hear her yell behind me but close the door securely.

I run down the hall and onto the balcony, seeing Abe, standing back from the banister and reloading, capping, pouring shot then pounding wads atop paper loads, as a half-dozen shots light the darkness in staccato flashes from the saloon floor and their roars shatter the echoes of the first shots. These sound like revolvers, then again a shotgun roars and more shots overlay each other so no one could figure how many.

I sidled up to Abe who's stepped back into shooting position, and before I can ask, he yells, "Hell, there must be a dozen of them. They rolled in a couple of axles from a freight wagon, even while trading lead with Colt. Get down, you're a target."

I hear footfalls on the stairs and hunker down and wait. Two of them top the stairs, side by side. At twenty feet I know the shotgun loads will take them both, and don't wait. We'd left a couple of coal oil lamps burning on the faro tables, but it's dark as a foot up an oxen's butt on the balcony, and they never see who kills them. I'm sure they're dead before they've rolled over backward to the bottom of the stairway.

"Colt?" I yell to Abe.

"Saw him go down right after he fired his second load. I surprised them from up here."

Moving to the head of the stairway, I slip up on my knees so I can see between the banister spokes and see a half dozen still intent on hauling Victor out. They are tipping the big safe over onto one of the thick oak axles. Were I not so busy I'd laugh as the thick oak axle breaks in half and the safe goes flat on the floor.

I recognize one of them, gimping on a peg leg, shouting orders at the others. Ian Burnie, the man whose lower leg was dumped in a garbage can thanks to my well-placed shot. I raise the Colt to finish the job when the railing next to me shatters and fills my cheek with splinters. Then recovering enough to see out of my left eye, I roll over to the head of the stairs. I'm on my belly so make a small target which is a good thing as the next to hit the stairway has a revolver in each hand and I know him to be handy with either. Sudden Sam, the shootist. Now dressed in all black he'd be a tough target, had the dim light of two coal oil lamps not been at his rear.

Unless shamed or forced, I would never face him if all was equal, but I have the advantage with darkness at my back, him picking his way up the stairs. Even though I only have six shots to his twelve, I don't believe I'll have to worry about the odds. I lay down on him, unseen, as he's charging up the stairs. I want him halfway up so there's no missing, but again don't have to worry as a scatter-gun to my right nearly blows my eardrum away, and lights the night with its muzzle flash. White gun smoke has filled the air so I can't see if Abe's aim was good...but I can't imagine it not being at that range. And moans from a man tumbling down stairs affirms that.

It's good enough that there's no return fire.

I chance peering over the banister as Abe again reloads, but now only see the fat backside of Ian Burnie elbowing his mates out of the way as they all scramble to get through the batwings as they've somehow gotten the thick security doors open. Which they must have done in order to wheel the safe outside.

Taking the stairs three at a time I have to leap over Sudden Sam, now only a former shootist, and sidestep the two I shotgunned...the three of them now a pile of bloody flesh at the toe of the stairway. I'm outside and see they've put a half-dozen six-by-sixes together to take the weight of Victor. I can hear the rattle of a heavy freight wagon and hoofbeats disappearing in the darkness. As I'm afoot there's no chasing them. Turning back, I have to step over a body on the planks of the street, and recognize a Wallaby I know as Otto Prager, Ian's right-hand man. He's still blowing bubbles from a chest wound, but if I'm any judge he has few breaths left.

It's my friend and extraordinary shootist, Colt Barberosa, who runs the tables and works for Tennessee Tom that now worries me. I run behind the bar to see him on his back, unmoving, a still cocked six-gun in hand. I slip down beside him and at first think him fine as his eyes are open. But quickly realize it's open in death.

I close his eyes for him. My breath catches in my throat, now burning like I swallowed a hot coal, and I bow my head for a moment and ask the good Lord to welcome this good man who'll make one tough angel at the right hand of God. He has the shotgun lying beside him. I round the bar, remembering Beth up in my room, and start for the stairs then realize four men, Wallabys I presume, are scattered around the room. One is sitting up, both hands covering a belly wound. Another is rolling back and forth, trying to get a belt to stop the bleeding in his thigh, while also holding a shoulder wound. Two are unmoving, one shot dead center, a hole in his chest as big as my fist, the other has an eye blown away and the back of his head is missing.

Had I, unfortunately, not seen so much blood in my short life I'd be sickened, as it is I'm merely saddened. Greed is man's second most deadly sin, after lust. And I see far too much of both in this devil's work I now do. More and I yearn for the farm with a day's task before you and few surprises other than weather and pests. On the farm you can look behind you and see what you've accomplished hour after hour, day after day. In the saloon and brothel, you merely look at a growing pile of gold coin. I guess that's an accomplishment of sorts, but I don't feel it's doing God's work, and my ma always said God's work has its own rewards.

I go from man to man and collect the handguns lying about, as Abe descends the stairs.

"Watch 'em," I warn, "they may have hideout guns."

He looks concerned, and asks, "You're bleeding. You get knicked?"

"Face full of splinters. Dig 'em out later."

I gather myself before opening my apartment door, then step inside. Walking through both rooms and out onto the deck, I'm both saddened and gratified...I guess a little confused...that Beth has disappeared.

29

By THE TIME THE COPPERS HAVE CLEARED OUT, HAULING the wounded with them, it seems I can still get an hour, maybe two, of sleep before I'm up against a new day. The good news tonight is Beth's concert and that should be some worry but a lot of pleasure.

But I don't sleep. I go through the trials and tribulations of the past few days. A burned-out storefront can be fixed; hopefully enemies, Chinese and Wallabys, can be or have been dealt with. All now know The Piccadilly can't be bullied. Try and you get more than you give.

That said, Juliet, our missing lady, is, like all of us, a person unto herself and that self is irreplaceable. Yes, we can hire another beautiful sporting lady...but that's hardly the point. We'd be more than a little concerned if it was any employee, friend, or even merely another human...but all of us are becoming like family. We need to find Juliet, help her if we can, avenge her if she's beyond help.

I never thought I'd find myself a "caretaker" of a bevy of sporting ladies or the overseer of more than a dozen employees...or even the resident of a burgeoning city. Truthfully I often yearn for the quiet of a high pine and fir-covered mountaintop where the sound of a clattering beer wagon is only a memory, or even for the quiet pleasure of following a mule while furrowing an arrow into a straight row soon to sprout corn higher than my head, each stalk yielding four or more juicy ears of nutritious corn for both our table and our stock's troughs...or to sell to those who don't grow their own. I made a commitment to Lord Stanley-Smyth, who's been my benefactor for more than two years, and above all I was taught to honor my word and commitments, but I miss my Oregon home and farm and family and plan to return as soon as my obligations to my benefactor and mentor are satisfied.

Stanley-Smyth is due here in less than three months and, hopefully, I'll be off to Oregon with my pockets bulging with a nice bonus for a job well done.

Beth joins Miss Alice, Tom, and me for our morning meeting. We have a Piccadilly family member, Colt, to bury and want to send him off in high style. We'll honor him by closing for a day so all can attend his funeral. He was well thought of and respected for his quiet competence by all, other than those he escorted out of the saloon, some with a boot to the butt. And the timing is bad as we also have Beth's concert tonight. She has come to the meeting, not to help me count, but rather to ask me to escort her to the Metropolitan at least an hour before the show, and to see if Tom can join us as additional security. It seems there has been talk of a disturbance due to the resident of a bawdy house performing at the city's most prestigious venue. I personally think it an outrage that a person's talent doesn't take precedent over her place of residence, particularly when a very young person whose residence is not of her own choice.

We're not closing for Beth's concert as our employees hear her at least twice a week as she performs from the balcony. And, hopefully, we'll have at least enough seats full to get my money back and pay Beth for her time and talent.

That said I've asked friend Barnabas along with two of his employees from Lord Stanley-Smyth's other local business, Kingdom Freight—hostlers who deal daily with thirteen-hundred-pound horses are pretty tough— to show up as additional security, and have hired four off-duty coppers, in uniform, just in case the rumor of a disturbance is true. Seven, plus Tom and myself, should discourage nearly any amount of unruly concertgoers. In fact, the thought of "unruly concertgoers" makes me smile, and possibly is an oxymoron, although I'm sure it would upset Beth.

We'll leave the house in the capable hands of Dodge, who I've come to trust as much as I have Tom and did Colt. I suggest an early supper and Beth, Tom, and I leave The Piccadilly with Barnabas driving Lord Stanley-Smyth's fancy coach, at five, stop at Nellies, one of my favorite short-order houses, where Beth orders a cup of bullion. She says the butterflies in her stomach couldn't handle more. We get lots of stares as she's already dressed for the stage. I have made reservations and promise her a triumphant post-concert supper at Desmond's Delmonico, where I haven't dined since Lord Stanley-Smyth picked up the tab.

We're all surprised to see more than a dozen folks in line at the Metropolitan, and it's an hour to show-time. The even better news is an angry mob has not gathered outside to protest; however two women are across the street carrying signs saying "No HARLOTS, No HOOCHIE SHOW at the Met." I manage to keep Beth from looking that way. The good news...looks as if I'll get my money back for sure, which makes me smile.

Carrying her violin case, I escort Beth through the backstage door. She's in another gown I've never seen, this one sea green, also cut modestly low, so full she has to tuck it in to pass through the doorway. She's wearing matching gloves nearly to the elbow, and heels maybe two inches high. I think she's put the gold coin thrown up on the balcony with each of her Piccadilly performances to good use. I'm surprised she's found a seamstress competent to make such a gown and gloves but must have as there hasn't been time for orders to arrive from Paris or even New Orleans.

Our young lady who arrived after losing her parents on the hard trip along the Oregon then California Trail, has blossomed into a woman, almost as beautiful as her aunt. And certainly, with better directed talents.

We are both surprised to see a sign on a dressing room door, *Elizabeth Deschamps*, with a big star below.

"You've taken your aunt's surname?" I ask.

"Not uncommon for a performer to adopt a nom de plume," she replies, opens the door, turns to me, and I'm not surprised when she says, "You'll excuse me. I'll touch up my makeup and relax a moment."

"I'll be close," I try and reassure her. And the door is shut in my face.

As I turn a tall man sporting a gold handled walking stick, slight graying at the temples below a high hat is upon me, extending his hand. "Prince Albert of Normandy at your service."

We shake and I'm tempted to say King Zane of

Oregon Territory, but don't. "Jake Zane, nice to meet you. Is it Prince, or Albert, or Al, or…?"

"Sir Albert will do," he says with lots of disdain in his voice. "I'm a partner in the Met, and other opera houses. An impresario, maestro, patron of the arts, and an aficionado of fine sopranos. Particularly world-class sopranos."

"You'll pardon my ignorance, sir, but isn't a maestro a musician or conductor?"

"It is, and I am. But my enterprise has expanded to presenter and representative of fine talent. I am renowned as impresario. I have pleasured the great cities of Europe with the talent I represent."

But not for your humility, I think, but don't say. I nod as if I know what the heck he's talking about, then add, "I hope you enjoy Beth's…Elizabeth's efforts. On the nights she performs we double the house."

"There's a great difference, young man, between a saloon squealer who flaunts her womanly charms, and a concert soprano. It was very supportive of you to rent the Met for your…your lady…but don't expect to bring down the house."

I smile knowingly. "Yes, sir. However, don't you be surprised if she does."

He gives me a phony smile. "San Francisco is no longer a bygone village. We've brought some wonderful—"

"Would you care to make a wager, sir?"

He flushes. Clears his throat, then answers, "I'm not a gambling man, sir, unless you consider betting on talent, which I do each time I book a show."

"Hope you enjoy my bet on Beth."

He nods, then asks, "May I meet the young lady? I just arrived back in the city—"

I interrupt, feeling a little testy with the popinjay prince. "She's resting." Just as I say it, we hear sounds of the violin being tuned up, so I correct myself. "She's practicing. You'll have time after—"

And this time I'm the one interrupted as he spins on a heel and stomps away, waving dismissively over his shoulder.

As he does, he passes the stage manager who's headed our way. I've met him before as he beckons me by name.

"Jake, tell the young lady the orchestra is tuned up, to your pleasure the house is sold out, and she's on stage in ten minutes."

"She'll be there," I say, and he reverses direction. I can't get the smile to recede with his "sold out" comment.

I reach up to knock on the door, and to my shock hear Beth sobbing.

30

WITHOUT WAITING FOR THE DOOR TO BE ANSWERED, I charge in. I'm happy to note she's sobbing and smiling at the same time.

"What?" I ask, rather taken aback.

"I'm so happy, Jake, I could just burst."

And again I remember my ma cautioning me, "Don't ever even try to understand women, Jake. The good Lord made us different for good reason. Wouldn't it be boring, no challenge at all, should we know exactly what the other person thought or would do, how they would react to our every move, which they also knew? A little mystery is the spice of life."

I laugh to myself and silently thank my ma, then charge forward. "Shall we walk to the wings?" I ask.

"Let me check my rouge. Have I tracked it with tears…happy tears?"

"As long as you haven't rusted up your vocal cords…"

She's at the looking glass, dabbing away with a cloth, then spins, picks up her violin, and takes my arm.

We wait in the wings while the orchestra plays

"Greensleeves." When finished the curtains part, Beth takes a deep breath, I whisper, "Break a leg," and she smiles and strides out. The applause is light and polite.

She taps her violin with her bow, then points it at the conductor. The orchestra plays a few bars then she steps in with "Old Folks at Home," a simple tune that requires little expertise, then she lets the bow hang from one hand and the violin from the other, and begins to sing, "Way down upon the Swanee River," and the crowd who looked as if they were about to yawn, becomes wide-eyed and many sit forward in their seats.

I think they are beginning to realize they are watching someone very special. The song was written as a minstrel and using the accent of Black farmhands, but Beth sings it pure, where Stephen Foster wrote "ribber" rather than "river," Beth sings the King's English. With hardly a breath between songs. When she finishes the final line of three stanzas, "Down in my good old home," and with barely a pause, the orchestra launches into the first bars of "Ave Maria." She sings the first verse in Italian, then repeats it in English.

> Ave Maria
> Maiden mild
> I listen to a maidens prayer
> For thou canst hear amid the wild
> 'Tis thou, 'tis thou canst save me amid despair
> We slumber safely 'til the morrow
> Though e'en by men outcast reviled
> Oh, maiden
> See a maiden sorrow
> Oh, mother hear a suppliant child
> Ave Maria

169

She stops, head bowed, then looks up, then when she's about to burst into tears, sad and shocked tears this time as the room is dead silent, the room erupts in applause.

Now her tears are tears of joy, but after a moment of thunderous applause, rows five and six of the center section, all women, begin to chant, "No harlot in the Met. Harlots out, that's our bet!" and they repeat it until the third time, when they are surprised by the rest of the house, a hundred sixty strong, and the orchestra, begin to boo.

Beth runs from the stage, into the wings, and throws her arms around me, tears streaming down her face. I think she thinks the boos are for her. I lead her to the edge of the wing curtains and show her as the protestors are surrounded by Beth's new fans who are escorting the women out, firmly, not gently.

"Can you imagine?" I say. "They are throwing them out."

In moments those who have led the protestors away have retaken their seats and another chant begins. This time it's "Elizabeth, Elizabeth, Elizabeth," and continues until I give her a small shove and she retakes the center of the stage. She plays and sings for another hour and a half, concluding with a difficult, but very popular Vivaldi violin piece, *The Four Seasons*.

I can see when the piece is complete, she bows but appears totally exhausted. She nearly collapses. I'm about to run onstage to make sure she keeps her feet, when the popinjay, Prince Albert, runs from the far side and offers his arm.

When thunderous applause quiets, he yells to the crowd, "Would you like to have Miss Deschamps appear again," and the thunderous applause is accompanied by shouts of "yes, yes, yes," and then, "encore, encore, encore."

The popinjay retreats and Beth locks the violin under her chin and plays, then sings "Ave Maria" again, bows deeply, and retreats away from me to the opposite wings.

The curtains close and I cross to the wings across the stage, where Beth and Prince Albert are engaged in intense conversation. I sidle up and interrupt, "Beth, we'll be late for our reservation."

She turns and gives me one of those devastating smiles, equal to one of her aunt's. "Oh, Jake, I'm so sorry. Sir Albert insists I dine with him as he has business to discuss." And then gives me her back and I watch them stroll away, her arm in his.

I see Miss Alice step up and trade words with Beth, but then she stands with mouth open, aghast I'd guess, as Beth and this Albert fellow depart. I call out to Miss Alice, "We're off to supper. You're invited?"

"I have a hack waiting. I'm exhausted," she says, and I detect tears beginning to fall. She walks away.

To tell the truth, my throat goes dry and I'm tongue-tied as Beth and the popinjay disappear.

"What the hell is that all about?" rings out behind me and I turn to see Tom approach.

I take a deep calming breath before answering. "It's about my buying you the best supper in town at Desmond's Delmonico. Is the coach out front?"

"Barnabas is never late. As soon as he saw those starched bitches heading for home with their fat tails between their legs, he's off to get the coach. Abe is with him."

I manage a smile. "Those starched old biddies kind of got their comeuppins, and from their own friends and neighbors."

Tom seems still amazed. "Did you caution that old crotch cricket who led Beth away that she has dangerous friends?"

"He ain't so old. To be truthful, I was so astounded she went off with him, my tongue froze like I was sticking it out at an artic norther. Princey and me had us a little tête-à-tête before, so I reckon he's aware. Let's eat. Dang reservations are hard to get." I act as if I've shrugged off her leaving with someone I know nothing about, but the fact is I'm shocked, totally dismayed, and a little confused.

As Blacks are not allowed in Desmond's, at least as customers, Barnabas stays with Abe and the coach as Tom and I take advantage of the reservation. I call a Black man over who's clearing tables and send a couple of plates out to Barnabas and Abe. I'd like to say what a wonderful meal it is, but everything seems a little sour to me.

I'm a little surprised when Beth shows up at our morning meeting, as if she hadn't just affronted us. Our take in saloon and at the tables was down last night, I presume many of our customers were at Beth's concert. I feel a little guilty about being gone as Kansas, one of our buxom barmaids, was cut by a customer. And my sponsored concert had taken Tom and Abe away. Dodge is included in our morning meeting as he was responsible for the place while we were gone. I must hire another gun who's willing to keep his gun stowed unless absolutely necessary and use muscle. In the case of Kansas, I would have condoned the use of a firearm as poor Kansas was cut from ear to chin by a customer, some cowardly som'bitch who called himself Orville Orleans. The knife wielder wanted her services as a soiled dove and took umbrage when she refused his advances. And of course, he fled like the coward he'd proved himself to be. What he doesn't know is The Piccadilly takes care of her own, and we'll not only pay Dr. Southerby to care for her—her initial care reported to be thirty-seven stitches —but for someone to track and bring this Orville to face justice. His future is not a sunny one.

Alex is due sometime today to take a report on the attack on Kansas.

Beth asks if I will stay for a few moments after Tom leaves. Alice remains. Normally Beth's presence would be more than welcome, but at the moment it rankles me.

31

Beth's first comment causes the heat to run up my backbone.

"Prince Albert is going to represent me, and you should know he insists I stop the shows here."

I turn to Miss Alice, who's normal angelic face seems as hard as granite. "And what do you think of this 'representation'?"

"I think we know little about this Albert, prince and prognosticator…or prevaricator, who's told her about all the fame and fortune he has for her. Elizabeth doesn't realize how beautiful and desired by older men she is. I have advised Elizabeth against making any harsh decisions. But he seems to have infatuated her. But not so much as she inflamed his lust."

So I turn to Beth, who I can see is angered by her aunt's comments. Her face has reddened. My tone is not gentle. "How much have you earned with that rain of gold coins each time you entertain here?"

But she ignores the question and is adamant. "I'll be

arranging for other accommodations, probably at the Niantic, today. I appreciate all you've done—"

"Appreciation," I snap, "is demonstrated, not mouthed, Beth. Talk is among the world's cheapest commodities. And your aunt and I only want what's best for you. How about you wait until we can get a report on Albert—"

"Prince Albert," she corrects.

"Aw, so you know his lineage. Or do you only know what he's told you?"

She's silent for a moment as both Miss Alice and I remain silent, awaiting her response.

And she does. "I've made up my mind. Prince Albert has a contract for me. He'll advance me one hundred dollars a month and book shows beginning with three or four at the Met then we'll go on to Chicago, Philadelphia, New York, and Boston, then Europe. He has a consort, Madam Hortense Twilloby, who'll travel with us and act as chaperone, my companion, and voice coach." She rises, gives us her back as she heads to the doors to the brothel. Saying as she walks away, "I have to pack. Please have my money available from the safe."

I call after her, "How about Mills Ladies College?" but she merely waves over her shoulder, dismissing me without comment.

After she's gone, Miss Alice asks, "She's only seventeen. I could appeal to the court and force her to stay should I be awarded formal custody."

I hate to dissuade her but am doubtful. "Please don't take this wrong, Miss Alice, but you're the madam of a brothel. There's not a pious judge, unless you can blackmail one, who'll give you custody of a young woman who's only a year from her majority."

Alice sighs deeply. "I'm sure you're right. It seems one

of the suffrages of life is we have to make our own mistakes."

I smile a little sadly. "Flat arse true. I know I've made my share of mine."

She manages a laugh. "And, young man, you've hardly begun. Just try and rack up more wins than losses."

"Good advice," I say, as she rises and follows her niece.

Life goes on, I think, and wonder, is Beth finding her own way a win or loss for The Piccadilly…and for me? I'll set out to find other entertainment, and cancel my negotiations for the mercantile next door, which I'd planned to turn into a theater. I hadn't mentioned that to Beth, not wanting her to be disappointed if I was unsuccessful. Now I'm glad those negotiations are yet to be successful. Our obviously fickle and unappreciative lead act would likely have left before the remodel was complete. Lord Stanley-Smyth advised me, "When you have an idea that will cost real money, savor it for at least a week or more before acting." I'm glad I've been savoring the merc next door for longer than that.

And I was developing a real attraction for Beth. Not only is she beautiful, and now turns out to be talented, but she talked as if interested in marriage and a family. It now seems I was hearing what I wanted to hear, not what she was saying.

"Sour grapes," I say aloud, but to myself, as I head for the stairway, seeing Alex enter through the batwings.

I catch up with him leaning over the bar. It's pretty early for three fingers of whiskey, but who am I to judge. He may have been working all night. With some apprehension, I ask, "Any word on Juliet?"

"Not why I'm here."

"Still a question…"

"No, nothing. We had twenty-three complaints filed by women at your whore's so-called concert last night."

I have to wait for the heat to leave my backbone before I answer, realizing I've balled both hands into fists. But I calm down before replying. "First, Elizabeth is not a whore. She lives with her aunt next door and works here three nights a week as entertainment. And, second, she got a ten minute standing ovation so some thought it a real concert. And, come to think of it, third, I'm sure the complaints filed are as wrong as you are."

He doesn't respond to that, so I mention, "You've got a button off your uniform?"

"Can't find a match or I'd replace it."

"Beth has a seamstress who's a real talent. Let's go next door. Maybe we can catch her as she's moving out… and get the lady's name and address."

I can see his face redden. "You know I won't put myself anywhere near that sodden, sorry, Godforsaken business of yours."

I shrug. "So, what's the basis of these complaints?"

"Assault. They claim they were accosted, molested, and manhandled when thrown out."

I laugh. "Filed against me?"

"And The Piccadilly and the Met. And we don't find this funny."

"Then you've lost your sense of humor, Alex. First, I was backstage. My arms are not twenty feet long. Second, the rest of the audience showed those old biddies—"

Alex's chin is tucked and his jaw clamps before he replies. "Some of the town's most prestigious women-folk. Including Marshal Willowby's and Judge Hoffman's wife."

I can't help myself but chuckle. The mayor has been a

Pleasure Parlour customer, but I'm discreet. "And the mayor's wife was among the unlawful demonstrators who disturbed the peace. I guess we should file a counter-complaint. The audience showed those old biddies to the door. No one working for the Met or for me or The Piccadilly laid a hand on them. I'll be happy to refund the cost of their tickets."

"Judge Hoffman will decide what happens."

I smile with only my eyes. Hoffman visits Alice's via the back door at least once a week. "So, Judge Hoffman's wife is a complainant and he's to judge the affair."

"I only enforce the law, Zane. I don't write it."

"So," I continue, "a hearing or what?"

"The ladies have retained Oliver McSwain who will be taking depositions from everyone we can identify who was involved or a witness, beginning with you and Miss Deschamps." He hands me two papers. "You've been served."

I glance at them. "One of these is for Elizabeth Deschamps. I'm not her."

"Watch your lip. I know you're not her. Is Thomas Throckmorton or the swamper Abe, unknown last name, on the premises?"

I hand Elizabeth's service paper back to him, but he doesn't take it. "I'm not her attorney, her representative, and no longer her employer. You'll have to handle this—"

"Zane, I once thought we were friends—"

"I've done nothing to change that."

He grabs the Beth service out of my hands, spins on his heel, and heads for the batwings. He waves over his shoulder. "Comply with the service or I'll be back to arrest you and others."

Then he turns back, again red in the face. "The rumor

around town is one of your whores made over two thousand dollars in dust in one night. Is that right?"

"My agreement with the girls and the dealers is never to disclose their income. Doesn't pay to advertise that kind of news. You know they already tried to haul Victor out of here."

"Victor?" His brow is furrowed with the question.

"Our big safe. You know damn well who Victor is. What's left of 'em that tried to rob us are in your pokey."

He nods, then asks, "When are you gonna plant Colt. I liked Colt."

"Tomorrow. Graveside at ten a.m."

"You better read that summons. You're to appear at ten a.m."

"We'll see about that," I say, and get a one-sided grin from Alex.

"You don't show and I'll be back to throw you in irons."

"Tomorrow's another day," I say.

"Humph," he manages, and pushes through the batwings.

I'm going to Colt's funeral, not some damn hearing. So, what to do?

32

RYAN ENFIELD IS A STEADY CUSTOMER OF THE PICCADILLY and, at the moment I'm happy to say, I hold a half-dozen Enfield markers totaling over one hundred dollars. And he's an attorney of some disrepute. As we are open and I don't want to leave again so soon, I ask Abe to run the lawyer down. With a ten-dollar marker in hand he's instructed to trade Enfield for a prompt appearance, so I can ascertain if he can make an appearance before Judge Hoffman on my behalf.

Enfield is as English as kidney pie and dresses as if he lived on London's Savile Row. That said, the scuttlebutt is he left London ahead of a fleet of bobbies who led a bigger flotilla of creditors. He landed on the Barbary Coast with two trunks and two hatboxes. It's rumored he shipped over a dozen pairs of shoes and boots.

He assures me he can make the appearance on my behalf and will be happy to do so with the surrender of another ten-dollar marker. It's an outrageous sum but I'm willing to pay so I can pay my respects and offer a proper farewell to Colt Barberosa.

We have a bit of a celebration this evening as the front of the saloon is closed in, sealed up, and secure as can be accomplished. Some finish work and painting is to be done, but she's closed up. The bordello is also enclosed, missing over ten feet of building on the street side, but canvas enclosed. Two rooms are missing as well as ten feet of the salon, but we're back in business. We've converted two dormer rooms in the attic for the use of the girls who lost the two rooms to the fire.

The lady's business is one that requires privacy, and the attic has become the fourth floor, the most private place in the bordello. To my surprise, those two rooms are fought over as the most prestigious rooms in the house. I guess because they are the largest and have a view from their dormer windows—not that I can imagine a view means much to the business that goes on in the ladies' rooms. But possibly also because of privacy. No one is peeking in a window that's four stories above the boardwalk.

As I think back on the past years, from leaving my spot on a big river in the center of these states and terri-tories where in the first month, at the age of fifteen, I became the head of the family. My pa died of the cholera and I was among other wagons in the wilderness on the Oregon Trail with two sisters and a mother to protect and provide for, along with a half-dozen oxen and two mules. Pa, in his wisdom, had hired an escaped slave, Sampson. A huge man as strong as the oxen we drove. He and I became the best of friends even though he couldn't speak. His tongue had been cut out by a som'bitch of an overseer on a Southern plantation, but his grunts and our sign language adapted. I've often thought had we been on our small farm where I had others to talk with, the necessity of our communicating would not have been so critical and I likely would not have developed such closeness. But months on the trail make fine fellows who depend upon each other for their very existence. Sampson was twice my age and I soon learned had a hundred times my knowledge about the flora and fauna, day-to-day work, and the quirks and abilities of the animals we take for granted.

We safely reached a new home near Oregon Territory's Snake River, thanks to a huge extent to Sampson. We reached that first goal far more wise, thanks to the greatest teacher, the wilds, and facing and living from the presence and availability of God's great variety of creatures. If you don't learn to harvest, hunger is a great and insistent teacher. You must learn from facing the weather, wild creatures, even dangers of your own making: heavy wagons, animals weighing near a ton, river crossings, disease, cliffs and crags you must traverse, and humans driven crazy by all the forementioned and more. Or crazy to protect their land and existence.

You soon realize if you don't learn and adapt, you die. That, in itself, is a teacher.

Most of the above relates to the physical but thank the good Lord I was blessed with a ma who concerned herself with the other great danger, and that is ignorance. She taught me that most of us are blessed with the ability to learn. Stupid is different than ignorant. Stupid means it's likely you can't learn because you don't have the mental capacity to do so. Stupid is also an unwillingness to learn. Ignorant is a choice. You don't learn because you don't take the trouble to do so. She taught us that curiosity along with the opposing thumb is the greatest gift God has bestowed on humans. Without wondering what and why, you don't learn.

My ma kept a dictionary under the seat of the wagon and when she didn't have the reins in hand, had that book and others. She grilled us daily about words, and we learned a new one and its proper use. Not only does the knowledge of words make you able to express yourself, but is important to learn what others say and mean.

She also fired math questions at us nearly every time we passed within earshot. By the time we arrived at the Snake we could all, even my younger sister, do our times tables through fifteens. And it's served me well since.

From the Snake I took a job sitting shotgun on a mule train hauling a load of gold from the territory to the new boomtown of San Francisco, where it could be shipped to London by its owner, Lord Stanley-Smyth. It was a learning experience to match the Oregon Trail. Most of the trip was without a trail other than that made by the critters who moved with the weather and availability of graze. A trail made by the critters that fed on green and the critters that fed on them. Including men. And many of those men took umbrage that we were in their homeland. You couldn't blame them for fighting to keep what they had, even though we had no intention of taking from them. They had no way to know that. I arrived in California with the cargo but without any of the mates I left the Snake with. Including the stepson of Lord Stanley-Smyth, whom I buried after an arrow through the neck called for a quick and shallow grave.

I guess I gained the confidence of that gentlemen, Stanley-Smyth, and his wife, by fulfilling my task. And more so when I retrieved the son's body—with the help of a squad of the California Guard—for proper burial.

Even though it was my intention to return to the farms we'd founded in Oregon, Lord Stanley-Smyth had other thoughts and I found myself unable to refuse his generous offer. I served aboard one of his lumber ships plying the Pacific coast for material to feed the growing town of San Francisco and then aboard one of his full-rigged ships sailing as far as the China Sea.

Again I came to San Francisco, ready to return to my family and friend Sampson in Oregon, only to be offered my position as the eyes of Lord Stanley-Smyth protecting his interest in a new venture, The Piccadilly, a saloon and brothel. A business he'd never have undertaken had his wife not gone to her reward. A business, like the ships had been, that was to teach me a whole new set of skills, and a position due to the Lord's generosity I couldn't afford to turn down.

So, here I am, about to face a charge for breaking the law. Another first for me. And like many firsts I've faced in the last four years, it's not really of my own making. I learned early on, from the death of my father, that fate cares little for your intent. What's important is how you act and react to what fate throws at you. The wilds teach you to adapt.

Adapt or die.

I've faced a lot of creatures who wanted me to die, some to feed on me, most as they protected their place in what was claimed as a place to live and thought me an interloper with designs on their place or very body.

But the most dangerous of those were man. Man can be a devious and clever adversary and no matter how feral and primitive you might think one, or a tribe, might be. They've survived weather, disease, and other men. Some groups or tribes have done so for eons. So underestimating them is a recipe for your own destruction.

And now I have to go before the law of a land, and its possessors, who have created laws for their own benefit. They'll protest and say they created laws for the benefit of all their brethren, but I know that to be a falsehood. Laws are, too many times, created for the benefit of the few.

Justice, true justice, is only a goal. Often not attained by law, even the law of the land, meaning those made by our founding fathers but remaining unfulfilled for many.

Coming to know, my friend Sampson taught me one thing. Slavery is a sin, a sin endorsed by the laws of the land. Laws that are being debated daily if the newspapers are correct. And cementing the fact law and fairness can be as far apart as the coasts of this new place called the United States.

So law and right are not always the same.

We'll see, come tomorrow, if the law is right in this particular instance.

33

COLT HAD MENTIONED TO ONE OF THE GIRLS THAT THE Mission Dolores Cemetery would be a nice place to be planted, alongside the city's old-timers, but as he'd never attended mass there or even so much as worn a Catholic medal of any kind, the priest there suggested Yerba Buena Cemetery, twenty acres over off Market Street. None of us had ever discussed religion with him, so we had no argument. By dawn we had a sign up on the batwings.

SALOON AND PLEASURE PARLOUR CLOSED
TO THE GENERAL PUBLIC.
OPEN AT 9:00 A.M. FOR MOURNERS FOR
EMPLOYEE AND TREASURED FRIEND COLT
BARBEROSA, BROUGHT DOWN IN HIS PRIME
BY MURDEROUS WALLABYS.
INTERNMENT AT 10:00 A.M. YERBA BUENA.

I guess they knew the drinks would be on the house as the place had forty mourners by 9:30. The hearse was parked just outside, a black affair with beveled glass windows pulled by two white horses with black feather plumes on their heads. Colt rested inside The Piccadilly, his polished oak coffin, covered with flowers, on a pair of sawhorses.

We pass out drink tickets to those who enter. One to a mourner. We even allow the stumblebums who claim to be dear friends of Colt's to enter. I'd hired a violin and French horn player with high hopes Beth would attend and bless Colt with a couple of hymns, but by 9:45 when we planned to walk behind the hearse the eleven blocks to Yerba Buena, she hasn't shown. At least they earn their remuneration by playing softly in the background as the shop's whiskey slides down throats of many who likely couldn't tell if the body in the casket was Colt or President Polk.

After enlisting six to carry the casket, I yell to the crowd, "Bar's closed. We're heading for the grave," and walk out. I am not surprised when all but ten or so scatter for parts unknown. I am surprised that over two dozen Chinese await us near the hearse, all dressed in white as I've noticed at Chinese funerals is their custom. Standing back among them is Jade and Lily, brothel employees. They, too, are dressed in ankle length white.

Even more surprised—I'm almost speechless—when the tallest of the Chinese strides over and extends a hand. It's Yi Wong, whom I traded unpleasant words with in Marshal Willowby's office.

"Mr. Wong," I manage, as we shake.

"It is my pleasure, Mr. Zane. I'm sure you are wondering...Mr. Barberosa and I have become friends since that little misunderstanding we had. And since a foolish young Chinese thought he would gain recognition and reputation by engaging in a gun battle with Mr.

Barberosa. Rather than shoot the boy down as he deserved, Mr. Barberosa clubbed him unconscious and delivered him to us. The young man was punished for his stupidity and Mr. Barberosa was offered a reward for his tolerance. He refused it and asked it be given to the transportation fund—"

"Transportation fund?" I ask.

"Yes. You may know if a Celestial passes his body is returned to China so he can rest in the shadow of his ancestors. The tongs often provide the cost." He clears his throat. "I should have asked permission for Mr. Barberosa's many Celestial admirers to escort him to his resting place—"

"No. I'm pleased, respect requires no permission... and know that Colt would be pleased. I'm not surprised I didn't hear of this incident. Colt was not a man to either crow or complain."

Mr. Wong—at my invitation—Alice, Tom, and I form a side-by-side line directly behind the hearse, following us are all the ladies from the brothel, then all the men—bartenders, dealers, our cook Lars, and Abe—and behind, again to my surprise, forms up a Chinese band. Tom, as usual, has the big Irish wolfhound on a short leash at his side. I'd more than once seen Colt sitting shotgun with the big hound's head in his lap. The band, eight strong, is mostly drums, but a couple of string instruments I'd only seen in the Orient. They play a dirge as we begin to plod along. Behind them are a throng of Chinese that have grown to over forty strong, some carry banners, one leads an unmounted horse, and a carriage with only a driver follows. Many of the Chinese wear white headbands. Two lead the Chinese but only a few steps ahead and they carry lanterns. As we walk my curiosity overcomes me and I ask Mr. Wong,

"Why white, why the lanterns in daylight, why some headbands?"

He speaks in low tones as we move along. "White is the color of Buddhist mourning dress; mourning relatives and official mourners wear white headbands. As we knew little about Mr. Barberosa we could only speak of his fine qualities and have assigned official mourners. The two lanterns bear the family names of the deceased, both only say Barberosa. Banners follow the band. Next would normally be twelve Barberosa family members carrying tablets listing the rank and titles of the deceased, followed by four men in tall hats who ward off malevolent spirits. Following them are two Buddhist priests in white, carrying staffs with the 'eight auspicious signs' of Chinese Buddhism. The fish, jar, lotus, mystic knot, canopy, umbrella, conch shell, and wheel of the law. They are followed by two Taoist priests with symbolic staffs."

I'm staring straight ahead and I guess he thinks not paying attention.

He asks, "Am I boring you, Mr. Zane?"

"Oh, anything but, I'm fascinated. Please continue."

So he does. "The carriage contains food to be sacrificed at the cemetery. Next comes a tall banner giving the whole obituary of the deceased. We knew little of Mr. Barberosa, so the tall banner has little writing, but I assure you that means nothing. He was well respected."

He clears his throat and goes on. "Then follows the chief mourner, which would be myself had you not honored my unworthy self to follow the honored body directly. A riderless horse follows, carrying the spirit of the deceased, attended by two mourners. Had we been in charge of the event, the hearse would follow rather than lead. The hearse would be drawn by six horses—"

I interrupt, "I hope you don't think I've dishonored—"

"Of course not. You don't know our customs." He nods, then continues, "And attended by mourners who are reflected in its windows. The open carriage following bears a portrait of the deceased framed by a large floral wreath. One of our finest artists painted Colt and the painting will be given to The Piccadilly should you accept—"

"We'd be honored," I reply, stammering a little. I'm gobsmacked by his explanation and have to ask why such a demonstration for a man they hardly knew.

"The foolish boy he spared was my son, who carries a banner honoring Mr. Barberosa," Wong says, his eyes straight ahead. Then he continues, "A banner and umbrella follow, the latter customarily presented to a popular official when he leaves a district, as Mr. Barberosa is leaving this earth. Tall banners mounted on the following wagon display poetic epitaphs reading 'A star has fallen to earth' and 'Your name is made famous by this bitter record,' normally flanked by the names of sons, nephews, and cousins of the deceased, who will carry on the family name and honor. As we knew of none, we rather wrote we hope many of his offspring, unknown to us but also honored, will carry on his name and honor."

I now realize the procession has grown to over a city block following. I silently shake my head. Colt is honored by dozens. I'll be lucky to have my face covered with a new, clean neckerchief when dirt is shoveled over me.

34

THE DAY BEGINS WITH A BLANKET OF FOG, SO THICK YOU'D think you fell into a bin of cotton, but quickly burns off, bone-soaking cold turns to coat-shedding warmth, and the sun blesses us with comfort and just enough breeze to tickle the skin. The weather and burying a friend make one aware of the sublime value of simply being alive. You take deep breaths and notice the occasional bloom of a bright yellow daisy in a window box...affirmations of life.

As we move up the planked road of the rapidly growing town, I'm assaulted with the sounds and smells of what some call civilization—I've come to wonder the value of that state of man's habitation. Crab pots boiling, a wagon hauling a load shoveled from privies, a tannery with the stink of hides, then a cart with a dozen varieties of flowers and another with fresh bread and sausages. Some of which I'd barely have noticed were it not for a friend leaving for whatever awaits his soul.

I have not attended a formal funeral since we buried my father on the Oregon Trail, a strong virile man in the prime of his life. It makes me think on the fact that life is tenuous and none of us knows when we'll fall.

When we arrive at Yerba Buena Cemetery, I'm pleased to see my friend and our physician Phinias Southerby standing alongside Peter Stanford, manager of Adams, and his wife Madaline. It seems Colt's quiet confidence and competence has touched many.

But I'm more than a little disappointed not to see Elizabeth.

I'm very seldom brought to tears but one forms in the corner of an eye when Thor, the big Irish wolfhound, inches up on his belly and while the minister I've hired rattles on, lays his head on Colt's coffin. Daily he sidled up to Colt for a scratch and a little praise. Somehow it says more about the man than anything the black-suited, overly loquacious preacher could.

I throw a handful of dirt onto Colt's lowered coffin, turn, and head for Lord Stanley-Smyth's coach with a feeling, like the claws of a cat raking my back, nagging at me. Juliet is yet to be found and, of course, we fear the worst. The coward, Orville Orleans, has yet to be found and punished if it's Tom or myself who get our hands on him.

As Barnabas is there with the coach, I offer Alice and Tom a ride back, but they refuse, preferring to walk the downhill trek back.

I'd noticed a tall man dressed in black, including frock coat, flat hat, tall boots, and a pair of bone or ivory-gripped revolvers in polished black holsters. He catches up with me before I mount the coach and extends a hand.

"Mr. Zane, I'm Lincoln Kane Barberosa."

We shake as I ask, "Barberosa? Related to Colt?"

"Older brother."

"It's good to meet you, sir. Please, call me Jake. Colt was like a brother to me. Would you care to ride with me back to The Piccadilly?"

"I would. It's my intent to avenge my brother. We came out from Missouri together. We had a falling out and hadn't written since he was working with y'all. I've been working in Monterey—"

"At what, if you don't mind my asking?"

"Colt and I were both proficient with any kind of firearm or blade. In fact, I taught him. I'd just had a reconciliation with my younger brother. I was a dragoon captain in the Mexican War."

I chew on that as we ride back to the shop. Barnabas is driving and Abe has mounted up beside him.

Turning to Lincoln, I ask, "So, Lincoln, what was your job in Monterey?"

"Friends call me Linc, and I'd be pleased if you would. I sat shotgun on gold shipments and worked as personal protection for Percy Montague, who is a prominent mine and shipping company owner."

"We're short a man, I'm sorry to say. Any interest—"

"I quit my job to come see my brother off. Blood is binding, far deeper than a falling out."

"Then you have another job if you'd like. Colt was paid four dollars a day plus a meal or two, if that suits you?"

"Suits me fine."

"As far as I know, all them involved in robbing us and firing their weapons are either dead, some at Colt's hand, or in jail, so revenge may wait a while."

"I've got time. Just so you know I may light a shuck soon as I even the score…"

"Revenge on your own time. I'll tell you the same as I

told Colt…keep them holstered unless someone's life or our property is at risk."

"I'm of the school you don't pull one unless it's necessary to use it. If I reach there'll be smoke in the air before y'all can yell out." He smiles. "It doesn't pay to kill your customers. I've only had to reach once in over a year in Monterey."

"Good, then you're our man, presuming the floor and saloon manager agrees."

"And he is?"

"The tall fella in a flat hat like yours. He walked away with the lady, Miss Alice, who runs the bordello."

He gazes out the coach window for a moment. "I've seen him somewhere before. He got a name?"

"Tennessee Tom Throckmorton, worked the steamboats on the Mississippi before hiring on here."

"That's it. I saw him drop a couple of highbinders when coming downriver. One he shot face on, the other I thought unnecessary as he was trying to run. But I don't judge another man's trouble."

"I've found Tom books no threat. He's pretty much kept 'em holstered while working for us. You should have no trouble getting past Tom."

He's silent another moment, then asks, "Who would 'us' be?"

"The owner of all, lock, stock, and barrel is Lord Stanley-Smyth, over whose affairs I'm watching, merely as an employee, whilst he's away in New York or London."

He clears his throat, then says, "You don't mind my saying so, you seem young for all that responsibility?"

I smile. "Yep, young, just turned twenty. But, as Lord Stanley-Smyth told Miss Alice, I've had enough blood on my hands to be fifty and I've seen not only the elephant, but half the critters in and on and more than half the lands bordering the Pacific. I've got more miles on me, land and sea, than most twice or three times my age."

"Experience counts," he says. "I was a dragoon marching to Mexico younger than you," then is quiet the rest of the way to the shop. As we dismount, he suggests, "I'd like to let Tennessee Tom eyeball me soon as possible so I know my fate."

"He's walking back with Miss Alice. We keep a pot of red beans and rice and a pan of cornbread going day and night. Abe is our swamper and a trusted employee. How about you head for the kitchen with Abe and we'll join up when Tom returns."

"Suits me," he says, "my navel is scraping my backbone," and sticks a hand out to shake with Abe. I'm pleased to see that as you never know which way a Missouri man will jump, north or south of the Mason Dixon. A man sympathetic with slavery would never shake hands with a Black man. We have enough conflict in a gaming house without folks worrying about color or place of birth.

I enter and head for the stairway when a voice rings out, loud and demanding.

"Hold up, Zane. You're under arrest."

I stop and turn to see Alex and two other coppers at the batwings. It comes to me that my expensive attorney was not successful.

"For what?" I ask.

"You know for what. You were served and didn't appear in front of Judge Hoffman."

"Didn't attorney Enfield appear?"

"He did, however it was you served, not Enfield. The judge issued a bench warrant."

He waves a paper at me as the three of them cross the room.

"Hold on," another voice rings out, and I see Tom and Miss Alice have entered behind the three.

Alex turns to see Tom loop his coat behind his revolver, a move that says I'm ready to draw. It goes very quiet in the place.

"This is not your affair," Alex says, but his tone is not so adamant as it had been.

This time it's me that yells, "Hold on!" And I add, "I'll go in and take care of this. Tom, please run down my attorney, Ryan Enfield, and tell him I'm arrested."

Alex moves forward, wrist irons in hand.

"Is that necessary?" I say. "You know me. I'm coming peacefully."

"Standard procedure," Alex says, with too much satisfaction in his voice as he clamps on the irons.

And I'm off to be paraded up the boardwalk, I presume directly to the city jail, with a dozen occupants who'd like to filet my liver.

35

I TRY TO FOLLOW MY PARENTS' TEACHING, AND ALL THEY believed in and taught. The Bible, the basis of their beliefs, is contradictory, or so I've concluded. That does not mean it doesn't have centuries of knowledge to absorb. But its most basic tenant is a simple one, The Book of Luke as I recall, "And as ye would that men should do to you, do ye also to them likewise." It's normally called the Golden Rule, and normally quoted, "Do unto others as you would have others do unto you." The Golden Rule, which raises it above all others.

But there're times when it can be applied in a negative manner, as I do now as I'm paraded up the low rise toward the jail. I'd like to do unto Alex as he's doing unto me. Maybe lead him with one of Thor's leashes.

Ma taught me it's a valuable trait to set aside anger and not let it affect your thinking. Think logically, not with a mind cluttered with spite or vindictiveness.

Luckily, we head straight for the courthouse. I'm seated outside the court in a hallway, still shackled, while Hoffman finishes other business.

Then Alex has me stand and leads me inside. The judge is not at the bench, so we're seated in the first row for another fifteen minutes. Then a bailiff in a city copper uniform orders us to stand and the judge enters, takes a seat behind the bench, high enough to overlook the whole courtroom, and raps his gavel. He adjusts a pair of pince-nez glasses on his long nose, and eyes me.

"You're Zane?" he asks.

"Yes, sir. We've met before."

I can see the when and where we've met is something he'd as soon leave out of the proceedings.

He asks Alex, "Officer, if that man is shackled get them off him."

And he scrambles to do so. As I'm rubbing my wrists, I thank him. "Appreciate that, Your Honor."

"What's Mr. Zane doing in my court and why is he shackled?"

Alex now looks a little sheepish, but answers. "He's here as a witness in the matter of the ladies being manhandled at the Met. You signed a warrant, Your Honor, when he didn't show after being served?"

The judge glares at the bailiff. "Rotterman, didn't his attorney appear—"

Alex speaks up, "The warrant wasn't recalled, Your Honor."

Then the judge glares at Alex. "Weren't you in court when Enfield appeared on Zane's behalf?"

"Yes, sir."

"So you know we rescheduled Mr. Zane for a week hence, and you should be smart enough to know the warrant was, consequently, recalled. Even if my incompetent staff failed to make same clear. True or not?"

"I'm no attorney," Alex says, his tone a little too strong.

"Your Honor."

"Beg your pardon, Judge," Alex stammers.

"You'll address me as Judge or preferably Your Honor."

"Sorry, Your Honor."

Hoffman clears his throat, then with eyes like daggers, asks, "Tell me why, Deputy Marshal, you shouldn't spend a few days in our jail, dragging an upstanding citizen through the streets when you know a warrant had been recalled?"

"Sorry, Your Honor. As I said, I'm no attorney."

"Don't let there be a next time."

"Yes, Your Honor." Alex looks as sheepish as an old ewe with his eyes lowered.

"So you'll remember, I'm fining you two dollars. Pay up or do two days in jail."

"I have it right here," Alex stammers.

"Did I hear you right, Deputy?"

"I have it right here, Your Honor."

"Pay the bailiff."

"Yes, Your Honor."

And Alex digs some silver out of his pocket.

Hoffman turns to me. "Mr. Zane, please accept the court's apology."

"Thank you, sir...Your Honor," I say.

"I'm sure this ridiculous matter will be settled before you're expected to appear, so check with the court the day before."

"Yes, Your Honor," I say. "By the way, I offered to refund the cost of the tickets to the ladies."

"You're free to go," he says, without more comment.

I give him a nod and head for the door, where Tom and Abe await.

As we head back, Tom informs me he's talked with

Linc, Colt's brother, and has no problem having him fill the job.

We've reopened for the rest of the day, and I'm surprised to see Miss Alice and one of our dealers, Flaco Comacho, waiting on the front steps. Alice has Mugsy cradled in her arms, is stroking her fur, and tears roll down her cheeks.

"Mugsy alright?" I ask, at first thinking something amiss with my cat.

"Yes. Friend of Flaco's found Juliet...the worst, as we feared."

"Where?" I ask.

Flaco replies, "On the Pacific side, beyond the Presidio. Her body was covered with pine boughs from the windblown trees. The most northerly group of those pines, near the passage."

"Has anyone informed Willowby's office?" I ask.

Flaco speaks up. "No, señor. She was found by Mexicano compadres of mine, who fear the law. One of them, who has visited me at the tables, and had the dinero went to the sporting house, knew of her employment there and came to me."

"Can you take me there?" I ask my skinny Mexican dealer.

"Of course. But promise we will not involve mi amigos who discovered her and shooed the crows and vultures away. Mi amigos already have their trouble with the marshal's office."

"No problem. I'll tell them we received a note." I turn to Alice. "Please wait at least forty-five minutes then send Abe to report the discovery to Willowby's office." Abe has appeared, so I instruct him. "Go by Barnabas's and have him deliver two riding horses here for Flaco and me, then go on to Willowby's office, but make sure we have at least thirty minutes head start."

Abe shrugs, but strides away.

In less than fifteen minutes one of Barnabas's hostlers arrives, riding a mule, leading two saddled riding horses.

It takes Flaco and I nearly a half hour to find his friends a quarter mile down the beach from the end of the road, who leads us to a copse of windblown pines. Her rotting odor assails my nostrils long before I see her. Her location is exposed by crows, gulls, and a vulture taking wing. They've covered Juliet with a couple of serapes, but the clever crows have pulled them away, and I'm sickened by the fact they've eaten her eyes and pecked and torn away her cheeks and lips. And even more so they've had at her entrails which are spread about as only a mad killer might do. I contain a retch, only getting a slight burn of bile in my throat.

I'm not surprised to note her underwear, her knickers, are in place and what appears to be rope burns or shackle marks redden both her wrists and ankles. There's matted blood in her formerly beautiful blond hair, on the right side. I gently probe with a finger and feel the recessed skull. She's been bludgeoned hard enough to crush her skull, hard enough to kill her with that single blow.

I make a careful perusal of the underbrush surrounding her and find nothing of interest. Not even wheel or horse tracks. But it's been some time and with the constant wind and soft sand, I'd be surprised to find anything. Flaco, who carries a gold watch, folds it and slips it back in his watch pocket, and informs me, "The coppers will be arriving soon. Maybe we should step away so they don't accuse us of anything."

"True," I reply. "Seems my old friend Sergeant Alex

might arrest me for blocking the wind. Let's cover her up so the critters don't molest her even more."

As I'm gently placing the serape over her face, I notice something I hadn't seen before. Through her ripped and tattered cheeks I see something in her mouth and reach down, open it carefully, and remove the object.

"Damn, that's more than strange." I hand it to Flaco. "You ever see a button like that?"

"Sure, it's a button, lots of coats have big buttons like that."

"But not lots of mouths. I wonder if she didn't put it there hoping to help us find her killer. Or if she ripped it free of his garment, to hide it for us to find."

"Like I said, lots of coats—"

"Damned if they don't, but I happen to know a fella who hates whores and has a coat with buttons to match...and one's missing."

36

I CAN SEE IN THE DISTANCE THE COPPER'S WAGON PARKING near where we've tied the horses, and five coppers dismount and stride our way. As they near I can see they are led by Sergeant Alex O'Toole, who has suddenly become my nemesis.

He does not extend a hand when he approaches.

Rather, he snaps, "What the hell are you doing here?"

"She was my friend and employee. Word came to us at the shop, and we came straight here."

"Came from who?"

I shrug. "It was a note, left under the door."

"Where's the note?"

"Sorry, have no idea. I'll ask around and see if someone hung on to it."

Alex snarls at me. "That's why you damned laymen need to stay out of marshal business. Where's the whore?"

I stall him a moment. "I see you still haven't gotten your button replaced?"

"Not important, where's the whore?"

"Sergeant O'Toole, I'd appreciate it if you spoke more kindly of my departed friend."

"And I should give a good old country crap about what you appreciate. Where's the whore?"

I dig in my waistcoat watch pocket and fish out the button. "This looks to match the others on your uniform jacket."

He reaches out to take it, but I pull it back.

It confuses him for a second, then he snarls, "What? You want to get paid for the button?"

"I didn't buy it, I found it."

"Then give it over. We have more important business to attend to."

"You didn't ask where I found it. I believe I'll hang on to it and discuss it with your superiors."

"Discuss what?"

"The fact I found it where Juliet obviously hid it. I think likely hid it to let someone know who murdered her."

His mouth drops open. The four coppers with him are standing near, now with open mouths.

Then Alex blows up like a puffer fish, throwing his shoulders back, and stammering. "What...wha...what the hell are you saying. Where did you find that button. Hell, there are hundreds if not thousands of buttons just like... Where'd you find it?"

"Juliet had it in her mouth. I think she put it there after a tussle with her attacker. Put it there hoping somebody like me would find it."

He turns to his chums. "Take that button away from this whoremonger. This lowlife—"

One of his men is staring at him, and says in a low voice, "Nobody I know hates soiled doves like you do." Then he turns to me. "Mr. Zane, hand over the button. I swear I'll pass it and all that's been said here to Marshal Willowby."

Alex is getting red in the face and pounds a finger into the other copper's chest. "You work for me, and you'll do what I say or you'll be pounding the boardwalk looking for another position."

"We'll see," the other copper says, and steps forward with his hand out, palm up. "The button?"

I relent and hand it to him. "I'll trust you with this," I say, and give him a nod.

"To hell with all this foolishness. Where's the whore?"

I let Flaco lead them to Juliet.

I'm both sick at heart and sick to my stomach. To see a beautiful woman reduced to carrion is an addition to my life's experiences I can do without. To be certain a former friend, an officer of the law, is responsible, is heart breaking. And probably responsible for the murder of a half-dozen sporting ladies. After this morning's dealings with the court, I have renewed faith in the legal system. Now we'll see if it takes umbrage and is as incensed with one of its own being the most heinous kind of lawbreaker as I am. The Piccadilly and Jake Zane will make sure Juliet is revenged, but only if more proof of his involvement is ascertained. Again, I wish I was in Oregon behind a mule plowing a straight furrow I can be proud of. More and more I think cities are on the bottom rung of a barrel of privy leavings. Why is it when you pile folks together the worst of them seem to float to the top, like pond scum?

For the first time since I had my first mug of grog, I think I'm going to see if there's any value in getting what one of my bartender's calls pie-eyed, or plastered, or in one's cups.

I don't wait for Flaco, but head for my mount and for

Barnabas and Kingdom Freight and Mail to return the riding horse. Unlike The Piccadilly, the freight company is open around the clock, but Barnabas informs me he's put in his ten hours and he thinks it wise he accompany me on my stated goal of drinking the scene of seeing Juliet out of my mind.

We decide to visit every doorway that advertises whiskey and ale between his place and The Piccadilly, and do so.

We reach the shop just as Tom is closing. He and Barnabas help me up the stairs and drop me in my bed, only pulling my boots off.

As usual, Mugsy jumps up to join me in slumber, but I'm surprised when she snarls at me and jumps from the bed.

"Traitor," I mumble, and shut my eyes, but the room is spinning like a Missouri twister, and I have to open them again to quiet the storm, then put a foot out flat on the floor, then, the gall rising in my throat says to head for the privy out off to the side of my deck.

Bouncing off the walls, I barely make it before I bend over and empty my stomach, filling my nose. I have to close one nostril with a finger to blow the burning chunks away, then the other. Finally, I drop to my knees and decide the smelly opening to the basement two stories below is going to be my best friend until my gut decides it wants to live in quiet unison with the rest of my body.

I'm a half hour before I stumble back to bed but take my white washbowl from under its matching pitcher with me and park it on the floor, just in case my rankled stomach finds another mouthful of that hateful taste to rid itself of.

I come to the conclusion that rum is really the demon

many teetotalers proclaim. If another sip never crosses my lips, I'll not be unhappy.

Tomorrow is another day and hopefully I'll be able to navigate it. My first business is to see if Marshal Willowby takes the "button" as seriously as do I. If not him, I'll appeal to Judge Hoffman. Judge Hoffman who, Juliet confided in me, she called her Romeo, and who visited weekly. But, of course, in the most surreptitious manner.

The law is about to be truly tested.

37

OUR MORNING MEETING TURNS OUT TO BE A GATHERING of the clan. As I finish the normal with Tom and Miss Alice, I see Abe and Linc waiting for a turn at me.

Linc moves to my table first and I wave him to take a seat.

He begins without preamble, "I'll not let this interfere with my duty, but I'd like to know who was among those who tried to rob the place when Colt was killed?"

"Wallabys," I say without hesitation. "Sydney Ducks, the worst of them. Australians…"

"I know the scum. Monterey had her share."

"The only one I recognized that didn't end up with the digger was their peg leg leader, Ian Burnie. He's a guest in the city jail awaiting trial, so," I say with some caution in my voice, "out of reach of personal vengeance."

"Humph," Linc manages. Then asks, "Anyone else?"

"All dead, vengeance taken thanks to Abe with a little help from my Coach gun."

"And I thank you for that. And thanks for the info. I'll go to work," and he's on his feet striding way.

Abe quickly takes his place and sits without an invitation. Abe normally has a hint of a smile continually, as if amused by the world. But now his dark brow is furrowed and the big hands he rests on my table are clinched.

He begins without so much as a "good morning."

"Lil' Miss Juliet was kind to me, Mr. Zane. Mo' kind than any white woman in my whole forty years."

I smile and nod. "I noticed she welcomed you to her room more'n once."

"Many of the ladies next door figured it was bad for business should they allow me to keep company with 'em. But not Miss Juliet. Is it true that copper, O'Toole, kilt her?"

I explain to him exactly what had transpired with the button, how often Alex had proclaimed his hate for soiled doves, and that I was convinced he was Juliet's and others murderer. Then I added, "But we should let this play out with the law."

He studies me for a moment, then nods. "So long as the law figures to stretch his neck, fine with me. My anger will last like one of them barnacles on the dock down at the waterfront. It ain't going away. I just hope they gets it down afore my mad done boils over."

"So far San Francisco law has proved to be swift and decisive. No reason to think it won't be this time."

Abe leaves seemingly satisfied for the moment. Now I want to do my part by making sure Alex, being a copper of some status, is treated just like any other citizen. I hope I've attained some respect in the community by running a fair, honest establishment among many competitors who were otherwise. I plan to test it with city hall as soon as they have time to have their morning coffee and have clear, hopefully honest, outlooks on the day.

I'll start with the copper boss, Marshal Watson P. Willowby.

Happily, I find a note awaiting me, delivered by a copper, that the matter of the women being manhandled —their words not mine—at Beth's concert will be settled with the payment of a refund for their tickets. I'd have settled for five times that amount, which only proves that the law at times bends with the wind.

I haven't had my suit and four-in-hand on since Beth's concert and it was months before that. But I brush it off and beg Lily to give my shirt a press. I head out to Willowby's office wearing it and a new bowler hat that's never seen my pate. I glance at a windowpane on the merc next door, seeing myself in what I consider a silly head covering...but the hat was a gift from Miss Alice so I grin and bear it.

"Nice hat," Willowby says when I'm ushered into his office. Were I not on such serious business I'd have laughed out loud, but I don't.

"Thank you. A gift so I'm obliged to wear it."

"I'm serious. The latest style. I'm sure that's all the way from England."

"Have you guessed why I asked to meet you?"

"I don't do a lot of guessing in this job, Zane. But I was given the button by the young officer...Mickleson... and he indicated you seemed to think Sergeant Alex O'Toole involved?"

I eye him for a moment. He seems to have dismissed the possibility. So I carefully add the only other possibly incriminating information. "I had a conversation with one of our other sporting ladies. Goldy is a level-headed lady, does her work, keeps to herself, doesn't gossip—"

"Get on with it, Zane. I care little about the history of your soiled doves."

"She was second into the alley the night of the fire. Juliet was first. Goldy saw a wagon disappearing to the south and thought little of it at the time. I later asked her if it was a delivery wagon or what? She said only it was black and she could see no advertisements. So this morning before leaving I asked her if it could have been one of your two paddy wagons. She sort of lit up, and said, "You bet. Looked exactly like one.""

Willowby sighs deeply and sets back in his chair. He clears his throat before commenting. "So, you have a whore with a button in her mouth. You have an officer missing a button on his coat. I'll give you it's a like button, like buttons on a thousand coats in San Francisco. And you have a wagon 'looks like' a paddy wagon or, hell, could have been a paddy wagon. That's it?" He seems to be waiting for my comment, but I have none, so he continues. "No one saw your dove climbing into or being dragged into this wagon. No one reported wheel tracks near where she was dumped." He's silent a moment, then continues. "Go back to your work, Zane, and we'll continue with ours. I'll let you know if anything turns up."

"I'll be standing by," I assure him.

Then he eyes me carefully. "I don't suppose you were out and about on the town after The Piccadilly closed?"

"Last night?" I ask.

"Last night," he replies.

"The day kind of took it out of me. Joined my cat, Mugsy, the first minute I could and didn't rise until Lars waved a cup of hot coffee under my nose. Why?"

"Your old nemesis, that Wallaby peg leg—"

"Ian Burnie?"

"One and the same. Someone called him to the bars on his cell window just before sunrise and shot him between the eyes."

"The hell you say. Can't say I'm sorry."

"So, you know nothing about it?"

"Maybe that's why I slept so well," I say.

"We'll likely figure it out. Lots of folks on the street even that early. Don't be surprised if one of my people come around to take your statement." And he sets and picks up a paper and begins reading.

So, I guess I'm excused.

I return to the shop feeling like one of my problems is resolved, probably due to Colt's killing and Linc's revenge, but still like my sails are luffing and I'm making no headway. I have my fancy bowler tucked under an arm when I push through the batwings. We're open, and I'm wondering why as I head for the stairway as only two customers lean on the bar and one is at a faro table.

Abe heads me off before I reach the toe of the stairs. "Maybe we can talk in your apartment?" he asks.

"Sure," I say, taking the stairs two at a time.

I hang the hat on its peg, peel the coat and tie off, before I turn to Abe. "What's up?"

"First, is the law gonna do anything about O'Toole?"

"I think I ran into a brick wall, but to be truthful I'm not surprised. The next step is to place what we know in front of Judge Hoffman. It'll have to be informerly, but that's fine. He'll see me as he knows I know where he hangs his hat when not with his missus."

"How about I gives you a few more items I found last night."

"Found?"

"How about my investigation turned up. O'Toole has him a little single stall barn and tack room out behind his place out on the east side...you can see the Pacific."

"So, you invited yourself to take a little look around?"

"Didn't steal nothing he ain't already stole." He rolls some items out on my table. Then continues as I study the collection. "O'Toole got himself a wife and two young'uns. With young'uns I figured no one would hide things anywhere young'uns might look, and knowing young'uns as I do that's anywhere they can reach. This collection was wrapped in that there scarf on a top shelf even his woman couldn't reach. That earring with the little gold nugget is one of a pair I gave Juliet—"

I'm more than a little shocked and have to interrupt. "She was wearing the match."

He gazes off, his eyes going wet, but he shakes it off. "I do believe that woven ribbon necklace belonged to Ruth of Sharon...Peaches. Them other bobbles, I'd bet my last nickel, belong to them other sporting ladies gone missing."

"He must have been keeping count by taking something from each. O'Toole had us all fooled. He's a madman, crazier than a peach orchard boar."

I'm quiet for a moment, then give Abe a nod and pat on the back. But then set back and think a moment before speaking. "Okay, Abe. You've done fine, now how to get this information to Willowby, or Hoffman, without getting you tossed in the hotel with bars on the window. It's not like I can say this evidence just wandered in here."

He stares at me a moment before speaking. Low and serious, he finally states, "If them law dogs is so stupid or crooked as to not punish a madman, there's those of us who will."

I nod and add, "He won't go unpunished."

"You damn sure is right about that," Abe says, with a return nod.

"Can I take this…this evidence?"

"Yes sir," he says. Then he has second thoughts. "You go tell them law dogs what I found and where I found it. You get that lawyer of your'n to go along and get some'n says they won't throw me in the pokey, then I'll come right at 'em with this and my statement where I fetched it from. That sound wise to you, Mr. Jake?"

I give him a smile. "Sounds like you shoulda studied the law, Abe. You wanna fetch Enfield here?"

"I will, Mr. Jake. You oughta know, I'm gonna hide out just in case you don't get no agreement from dem law dogs. Should dey come huntin' me, I'm gonna run come dark."

"That's wise, Abe. You hide out in my apartment. Should they not do what's right. You have to run; I'll send you with your pay and a bonus."

"You always been fair, Mr. Jake. I'm off to find that Enfield fella."

38

I've sent Abe to confirm an appointment with Willowby and he returns advising me to come on over. Linc has picked up Colt's habit of accompanying me when I leave. I never thought I'd have the need of a bodyguard, and don't think so now, but with the number of Sydney Ducks and Ian Burnie shot dead in the city jail, and I presume with the bounty on me still being offered, I'm not too proud to accept another gun at my side.

As we walk along, I can't help but question him. "You heard the leader of the group that killed Colt met his maker?"

He smiles, a little too broadly. "Damned if he didn't. Took one right between his ugly eyes, so I hear."

"I don't guess you'd know anything about who deposited an ounce of lead in his head?"

He's silent for a moment, then smiles again. "If I did, young Jake, it likely wouldn't be wise to talk about it."

"Keep it that way. Willowby or one of his investigators will be around digging for information. You and I are likely atop the list of suspects."

"He was no loss to the community, and I don't imagine they'll dig too hard. Someone," and he stresses the word, "did San Francisco a favor."

Now it's my turn to smile. "Dang if they didn't."

Enfield's office is on the way, and he's said to drop by on our way to see Willowby, and we do. Abe does not accompany me inside, nor does Linc. I want this meeting to be only Willowby and myself, after and if Enfield gets what I learn is called an immunity agreement. Which, to my only slight, Willowby agrees to naming myself and a party whose name is to be provided after the agreement is executed.

When it's done I thank Enfield and ask him to excuse himself. He assures me I'll get a bill before the week is out. As if I wasn't positive that would be so.

Willowby's cordial, curious but cordial, even sending his male secretary to fetch us both a cup of coffee. His attitude hardens when I tell him I have proof of who's been killing the doves. I open the scarf and roll its contents out on his desk.

"What's all this?" he asks.

"The earring matches one still worn by our lady Juliet when she was found. The necklace made of woven silk belonged to our girl Goldy. The others, I'd bet my bottom dollar, came from the bodies of the other doves killed."

"So, where did all this come from?"

"From Alex O'Toole's stable. Hidden high on a shelf."

He looks at me as if I'm as crazy as the religious nut who's named himself, Elohim…God. Who I owe a silent apology to for thinking he was the murderer.

Willowby stammers, "You don't…you don't think,

Alex...Officer O'Toole had anything to do with those deaths. The gutting of those girls?"

"I hate to think so, but no one hates whores more than Alex. He's said so many times in so many ways. He refuses to go into the brothel, he's refused to touch or even talk to the girls, even with Miss Alice who doesn't... at least no longer practices the trade. When Juliet went missing, one of our other girls thinks it was a paddy wagon leaving the alley behind The Piccadilly."

I'm more than a little surprised when he yells to his secretary, "Kenny, go find O'Toole and get him in here."

"This should be interesting," I mutter. We don't say a word to each other while waiting for O'Toole.

When he enters he gives me a disdainful glance. "What the hell have you done now, Zane. Hopefully something I can use to put you in the same cell with those Wallabys we're holding." Then he sees the items on Willowby's desk.

"What..." He mumbles, then looks from me to Willowby and back again. "What's this," he finally snaps, but I notice his face has reddened.

Willowby doesn't answer so I do. "You should know, those things belonging to more than a half-dozen murdered soiled doves were found in your possession. Your stable to be precise."

He is silent for a long moment, then the light seems to come on and he says, with confidence, "My cases. I've always kept something to remind me of the cases I'm working on. Each of those came from a case I'm actively working on."

Then something dawns on me. "See the earring. That came from our girl Juliet." I turn to Willowby. "I presume you keep the possessions of murder victims, at least for some time?"

"Of course, it's evidence."

"I've got a hundred dollars I'll bet to your dime; you'll find a matching ear ring...I know as she was wearing it when I saw her well before O'Toole was on the scene. He took an earring when he killed her. That one among those things. An earring in the evidence you're holding proves that one was taken long before."

"I'm not listening to this!" he yells at me, spittle flying. He steps back and turns. "I'm going back to my desk."

"No," Willowby snaps. "You're going home. You're on leave until we get to the bottom of this."

"Fine!" he yells, and stomps out.

When he's gone, Willowby looks as if he's been run over by a beer wagon. He finally says, "Thank you, I think. If he did this, he won't get away with it. It sickens me if true."

"And me, to think I thought of him as a good friend at one time."

"I'll keep you posted. You, and...by the way, whose name goes on this immunity agreement?"

"Abraham, the man of color who's our swamper at The Piccadilly."

"No last name?"

"If he has one I don't know it. The description will do. I'll have him come in and sign or make his mark if you'd like?"

"Not necessary. We'll be in touch."

And I'm excused.

When I enter the shop with Linc, Abe is working; he hurries over.

"Well?" he asks.

"Now we wait. I have an agreement that protects you from arrest so just go on with business as usual."

"Dey hang him, or I do," Abe says, his tone serious enough so I believe him.

"Let's let it play out. I don't want to see you hang instead of O'Toole."

"You gots a surprise," Abe says.

"I like surprises. What?"

"De big boss. He be over with Miss Alice."

"Lord Stanley-Smyth?" I ask, my mouth hanging open.

"Dat's de big boss. He be all smiles. I guess that be good."

"From your lips to God's ears," I manage, then head for the stairs to go next door.

Abe yells after me, "I gots personal business, be gone a while."

I wave over my shoulder, then stop and turn, concerned about what his business might be.

39

I'm only halfway up the stairs when Lord Stanley-Smyth bursts out the door of the brothel, with Miss Alice on his heels. We reach the head of the stairs at the same time, and he embraces me in a bear hug that almost takes my breath. Then he pushes away and stands with both hands on my shoulders.

"My young Jake Zane, you have exceeded my grandest wish."

"Tried only to do what you instructed," I manage.

"And much I didn't, but all meets my approval." He studies me a moment. "I fear I've aged you beyond the near year I've been gone. You have a few fine lines from wrinkling your brow. I presume with worry?"

I laugh. "I have lost a little sleep with the responsibility. However, I've learned far more than loss might touch."

He turns to Miss Alice, and I think surprises her a little with, "Jake and I will retire to his apartment to talk things over. You will excuse us?"

Miss Alice reddens a little but turns and retreats to

her lair. As we head for my rooms, Tom and Linc top the stairway and I introduce the Lord to Linc after he greets Tom, telling him Linc is Colt's brother and I'll explain how it came about that he's taken Colt's place.

Before we excuse ourselves, I ask Tom to tell Lars or Emma to bring us up a pot of tea, cups, and cream as I know how the Lord takes it.

We sit, laugh, and commiserate, as I relate the past months. As I suspected and hoped, he says The Piccadilly will pick up the cost of the Celestial girls' education. That's a major weight off my shoulders. In fact, we'll establish the Lady Stanley-Smyth Educational Fund for Young Women and continue funding it so long as he has business in San Francisco.

Which brings him to news that does shock me. He's negotiating to sell The Piccadilly and Miss Alice's Pleasure Parlour. His negotiation carries the proviso that Tom has first right on the saloon, and Miss Alice on the brothel. He also grants them each a thousand-dollar bonus and each of the other employees a hundred dollars each. As he doesn't mention I have any continuing rights or bonus, I'm a little taken aback. He's aware his accounts and the drafts forwarded to him now exceed sixty thousand dollars.

He thanks me for a job well done and rises, and I'm sure the disappointment shows on my face, but I stand, shake, and thank him for the opportunity and education.

"Now, about Jake Zane," he says, and my hopes rise I'll be entitled to some compensation beyond pay, opportunity, and education. Then I'm shocked. "You'll draw five thousand dollars for yourself."

My mouth drops open.

"You've earned it," he continues, then shocks me again. "I hope you'll consider staying in my employ."

"How so, sir?"

"I'm at the Niantic and would like you to join me for supper, say seven?"

"Of course."

"That'll give you a chance to think about your future—"

"I do need to visit my family—"

"Of course, a short visit I hope?"

I'm silent for a moment. Then offer, "I guess I should hear you out before I satiate my desire to be back behind a plow."

That makes him guffaw, then when he stops laughing, he says, "I'd be surprised, young man, if you're ever behind a plow again. You have far too much talent and common sense not to honor it with accomplishment. Far more than to return to breathing what a hardworking mule blesses you with as you follow." He guffaws again, and heads for my door. "Seven," he says, waves over his shoulder, but I stop him with a yell.

"Sir!"

He turns and I relate another piece of The Piccadilly business I'd nearly forgotten. "One of our barmaids was cut badly, from ear to chin by a customer while on the job. We know who the culprit was and I'd like to place a five-hundred-dollar reward for his capture."

"Did we pay her medical costs?" he asks, obviously concerned.

"We did, and I kept her on in the laundry and kitchen."

"Good, offer the reward." He closes the door quietly.

It seems it's my day for shocks.

I'm still trying to process the fact I'm to be in possession of more money than I'd ever consider having, when there's a knock on my door.

"A city policeman is at the door asking for you."

I head for the stairs wondering what now. A uniformed copper I don't know is waiting near the batwings. He doesn't waste time with formalities and merely hands me a written message, spins on a heel, and leaves. With only three at our long bar, I walk over and belly up to a space with others far away and unfold the parchment.

It's from Willowby. "I don't know whether to celebrate or bemoan this, but Officer Alex O'Toole was discovered by his wife. He hung himself in his stable. I presume this establishes his guilt but will never know for sure. He left no note. We are collecting a fund for his two children if The Piccadilly or you would like to contribute."

Had I not been scheduled for a supper with Lord Stanley-Smyth, I'd order a bottle of Who-Hit-John and soak my soul as I contemplated man's inhumanity to man, and occasionally to himself. Then another possibility crosses my mind. Abe has been missing, saying he had business to attend to. One can only wonder if O'Toole had some help with that rope? Abe has not returned. It will be interesting to contemplate if he does not return. He has money coming, near a week's pay and now a hundred-dollar bonus.

We have a quiet afternoon, with the exception of lots of chatter about Alex. Finally I head for my rooms and brush and dress in my good suit. Even as the social animal the Lord is, he's at a table alone when I arrive a few minutes before seven.

He greets me, standing and offering a hand, then saying, "You're always a little early, Jake. It's a fine habit and one that says to whomever you're meeting that you respect their time."

"My pa taught me that being late says you think your time more important than whomever your scheduled to meet. Starting a meeting being disliked is unwise."

He smiles. "Your father was a wise man."

"And I'm lucky my ma equaled his sagacity."

Again he laughs. "And taught you a good bit of the King's English. Now, to leave your country upbringing back in the country, from now on refer to your ma and pa as mother and father. It will serve you better in the sophisticated world I hope you'll enter."

"Yes, sir. Mother and father."

We make small talk for a while as we wait on the beefsteak he's ordered then when served, he clears his throat, and asks, "What do you know about India?"

Again, today, I'm taken aback. I chew my steak and digest his question before I answer. "To be truthful, not much. A very large country, densely populated. Poor, but with a rich history."

"A good start," he says, and reaches to the chair next to him and comes up with two books. He hands them over and I read the title, *The History of India* by The Honorable Mountstuart Elphinstone, in two volumes.

Before I can comment, he advises, "I'm going into the tea business and will have a couple of volumes for you on that subject. After you visit your family, return to San Francisco and you'll catch a ship to London. I'll meet you there and we'll spend a month there then leave for the Barak River Valley, the most eastern part of India in the shadow of the Himalayas where I've acquired two thousand hectares of land—only one hundred hectares currently in production with Assam black tea. The finest in the world." He awaits my comment, but I'm too stunned to talk. "The other nearly thousand acres lends itself to planting. You'll receive two hundred fifty dollars monthly remuneration, plus a five percent interest in the endeavor. When can you leave for a visit with your family?"

I'm still awestruck. As I've noticed with Lord Stanley-Smyth, he's an expert in what I've learned is an assertive close. It's a trait I've studied and know works to attain what you want. He wants me, and, as usual, has offered me an opportunity I can't refuse, and moved forward with the assumption I'm on board. But I can't help but ask, "Of course you know I know absolutely nothing about India or the cultivation of tea."

He laughs. "You're a farmer at heart. You'll run the operation, and like this job you'll have people with years of experience at your beck and call. Management is management and you've proven you rule with humility and, to use your term, sagacity. Take the best of those under you, apply good judgment, and all will be well. When can you leave?"

"I want a month with my family?"

He hands me an envelope. "A thousand dollars traveling money, addresses in London you'll need as well as names of administrators in English government and even friends of mine who'll assist you if you need help in any way. I'll see you in London in three or four months, or as soon as you can get there after a month with mother and siblings. Then we're off. You'll want to brush up on tigers, elephants, and the Hindu."

"London, three or four months."

I can't help but think, the Barak River Valley, in the shadow of the world's tallest mountain, is a long, long way from my birthplace on the Missouri River.

Halfway around the world.

A LOOK AT: SHADOW OF THE MAST

BY L.J. MARTIN

From the author of Two Thousand Grueling Miles and Rugged Trails comes a saga as wide and wild as the Americas.

From Boston to Old California, young Sam McCreed grows to become as hard and skilled as the friends and foes he works alongside and escapes into a land equally threatening and dangerous as the watery hell that brought him to her shores. A young man now hardened by fists, ice, sea, and lash, he escapes into a California that has become a caldron boiling over with danger and resentment. And McCreed, now an unequaled horseman, an expert with blade, musket, and reata, is a man on the prowl for vengeance.

Driven by a lust and love for a fiery-eyed, raven haired senorita, he'll send any man who stands in his way straight to hell.

AVAILABLE NOW

ABOUT THE AUTHOR

L. J. Martin is the author of 70 young adult, classic western, historical and thriller novels with a half-dozen non-fiction works among the mix. His first novel was a Y.A. and is still in print. As the father of four boys he was adamant about them filling their days with good books, books that taught values and how great the American experience is and was. He lives in Montana on a small ranch and winters in Prescott, Arizona, both homes in western areas steeped in history. Having wrangled, packed mules, farmed and ranched, sailed his own ketch, and studied history all his life, he's particularly suited to writing about what he loves, the west. He's lived among and studied its critters, ranchers, miners, soldiers, mariners, river men and townsmen and women, and their history. His most recent historical endeavor was writing/directing/producing the classic western film EYE FOR EYE, adapted from his novella of the same name.

www.ingramcontent.com/pod-product-compliance
Lightning Source LLC
Chambersburg PA
CBHW011435240626
47153CB00011B/2995